GOLDEN ARMOUR

THE HELMET

Prince Badrur watched impassively from the ridge. He knew that the superior might of his creatures would wear down the resistance eventually; but perhaps there was something he could do to speed matters along. He called to a dragon-like creature gliding overhead. It landed in front of him and folded its wings. "Your snout looks strong," said Badrur. "Is it strong enough to smash through the glass and frame of the Mansion windows?"

By way of demonstration, the dragon-like creature hit a nearby stone with its snout. The stone shattered. The prince was delighted.

"Break into the third window from the left. There you will find Lord Tancred. Tear him to pieces and bring me a mouthful of his flesh."

Also available in this series:

2: The Shield

And coming soon:

3: The Spurs
4: The Sword

GOLDEN ARMOUR

THE HELMET

Richard Brown

Hippo

Scholastic Children's Books,
Commonwealth House, 1–19 New Oxford Street,
London WC1A 1NU, UK
a division of Scholastic Ltd
London ~ New York ~ Toronto ~ Sydney ~ Auckland
Mexico City ~ New Delhi ~ Hong Kong

First published by Scholastic Ltd, 2000

ISBN 0 590 63775 4

Typeset by DP Photosetting, Aylesbury, Bucks.
Printed and bound in Great Britain by The Bath Press, Bath.

2 4 6 8 10 9 7 5 3

THE ORIGIN OF THE GOLDEN ARMOUR

In the midst of a treacherous sea, there is a tiny island. It is temperate and beautiful all the year round. But no one lives there, for it is bewitched. At the heart of it is a ruined temple – and a broken paradise.

It is all that is left of a vast island which Citatha, the goddess of nature, once reigned over. The climate was sunny and calm, and nature was always in balance. The temple at the centre of the island was magnificent then. Statues and pictures of the goddess were everywhere in shrines and alcoves, groves and gardens. She wore flowers in her hair, a robe made of lilies and a cloak sewn with a hundred different leaves. Graceful, silver-haired cats slipped in and out of the temple columns, like the spirits of past priestesses.

And then, catastrophe! A huge volcano spewed up masses of ash and lava. Its force was so great, it split the island into four. Tidal-waves poured over the land and vast tracts of Citatha's world fell into the boiling sea.

When the air cleared, she saw there was nothing left but four distant islands, shrouded in ash and full of death. Only

1

a fragment of her paradise remained, and in the ruins of her deserted temple, she grieved for her lost world.

In time, North Island became cold and bleak, East Island a burning desert, West Island a land of fogs, and on South Island the rain made the land perpetually flooded.

In sorrow, Citatha dreamed a great dream. Out of her dream there stepped a suit of golden armour, etched with many glittering patterns.

Citatha entered the Golden Armour and infused it with her magic. She imbued it with Nature. Then she left it to do its destined work.

It rested in the deepest vault of the ruined temple. The Helmet shimmered with frost. The Shield hummed with a hot and scouring wind. The Spurs were shrouded in mist. And raindrops glittered on the scabbard of the Sword.

For centuries it has waited there in that deep and sacred vault. Parts of it have by mysterious means found their way to the islands. There, hidden by time, they await the coming of those who can release the magic within them.

Only then will Citatha's reign be restored. And only then will the four islands become like the paradise they once were, beautiful and calm.

CHAPTER 1

Tara the wolf-girl stood in the shelter of an oak tree and shivered. The cold wind buffeted the tree-tops and crept icily through the undergrowth. In the forest clearing, the wolf-people had arrived back home, having served for a month as servants in the Mansion. They were milling about excitedly, yapping, licking, nipping, barking, rolling about in the leaves together. Tara watched them, sad and yearning.

Mingling with the welcomes were loud and tearful farewells. Those who were going back to the Mansion, as replacement servants, slipped regretfully out of their skins, and stood naked and shivering as humans in the frosty moonlight. The new arrivals seized their discarded skins and wriggled into them, a look of profound relief on their wolfish faces.

Tara had heard many stories of the Mansion, of the ways of humans, of their peculiar smell and lack of fur, of their cunning and mastery. One of the humans was now visible above the commotion. Aulic. He was standing on a sledge, wrapped in a great black bearskin, waving his arms about, shouting.

She watched restlessly, softly yapping to herself.

Circling the edge of the clearing, and averting her eyes from the scenes of reunion, she paused behind a log and watched Aulic. How ugly he was, how powerful; he struck an obscure terror in her. But humans fascinated her. She had watched them hunting and trapping: they seemed so slow and helpless on their two legs, and yet so dangerous.

Stepping from behind the log, she paused at the edge of the clearing, wondering what she should do. Naked wolf-people were clambering on to the carts and sledges, huddling together under deer- and bear-skins.

She had been told of the children of the Mansion, of Keiron and Cassie: two exalted human children with no mother and an eccentric father. She had heard how Cassie had often been there to welcome the new batch of wolf-servants, to warm them with kind words and see that they were settled in; and of how Keiron would show them through all the dark and twisting passages of the great house.

Aulic gracelessly accepted a horn of water from a wolf-woman, and gulped down the cold, brackish liquid. He flung the horn aside, swore at any wolf-person in sight and shouted at the more timid stragglers: "Get a move on. I'm not waiting any longer."

For some time now, Tara had had an obscure sense that she stood apart from her pack. Was she the only one who was reluctant to return to her wolf-skin? Who sometimes found her human form more beautiful than her wolf one? Often, she yearned to strike out into the dark forest on her own. But where would she go?

As she watched the wolf-people huddling under the furs on the giant sledges, ready to set out for the Mansion, an impulse rose up in her, a crackle of energy that made her leap up and yelp. She was much too young to serve in the Mansion, but that wasn't going to stop her now. She raced over the clearing towards the nearest sledge, even as Aulic was signalling for them to leave.

Tara heard voices behind her, calling her back, but she did not heed them. With one concentrated twist of her body, she shed her skin. She felt a pang of remorse as it slid to her feet, but she knew that it would be well looked after in her absence. Not pausing to look at her moon-white human form, she clambered on to the nearest sledge and slid under a pile of furs.

"It's not your turn, girl," voices among the furs said. "You're too young." But it was too late, whips were being cracked, horses were snorting, sledges were turning: they were on the move.

An hour later, they emerged from the wind-torn forest and struck out over rugged brush. Here the full force of the wind hit them, threatening to snatch away their mounds of furs. The horses struggled on, their heads bent, goaded by the sting of whips. Tara felt the cold envelop her; she pulled the dead skins tighter around her, realizing the mad sacrifice she had made in leaving her own skin behind.

At last they came to the top of a high, flat ridge, where the horses were allowed to catch their breath. Far away in the distance a cold, metallic sea glittered fitfully in the moonlight between scudding clouds. Below them, on the rocky coast, stood the Mansion, a sprawling, shadowy building, surrounded by out-buildings and a circling wall. Faint lights flickered in many windows.

They trotted the last stretch down to the house, the horses breathing heavily after their long trek.

The great gates of the Mansion opened to swallow them up. The wolf-people emerged from their sledges, blinking and apprehensive, jostling together uncertainly in a dank courtyard. No stories of the Mansion ever prepared them for the first shock of that dark and gloomy place of shadows.

Tara was in panic at being hemmed in and surrounded by looming walls and turrets. She hid behind a rotting water-butt against a wall. She heard Aulic telling them to enter the Mansion at once. She wanted to join them, but she felt paralysed with a nameless fear. She curled her strange, elongated body into a tight ball, wishing for her wolf-tail that it might cover her eyes.

After what seemed an endless time, she felt a warm hand on her arm and heard a soft, coaxing voice. She shrank back and opened her eyes.

A few minutes earlier, Cassie, the daughter of the Mansion, twelve years old, opened a window that overlooked the courtyard and leaned on the sill. She watched the wolf-people slip out from under the mounds of furs on the carts and hurry, suspicious and a little afraid, into the building. How ridiculous Aulic looked in that oversized coat!

The wind whipped her long, thick, ash-blonde hair into her eyes; parting it, she caught sight of the wolf-girl still huddled behind the water-butt. She craned to get a better view and saw, even from this distance, that the wolf-girl was trembling. Poor thing! And what was one so young doing here, anyway?

She ran down the stone stairs and hurried into the courtyard, just missing bumping into Aulic who was waddling determinedly across the flagstones towards the wolf-girl.

"Out!" he shouted at Tara, and when she did not immediately respond, he began to prod her. "Come on, out!"

"Let me talk to her," said Cassie. She pushed the man-servant aside.

She crouched beside Tara and said, "Don't be afraid. What is the matter?"

Tara looked into the girl's brown eyes and beautiful face and at once felt her trembling ease. She tried to answer but, although she had been taught from infancy to speak the human tongue, what came out was a sort of strangled yelp.

Cassie spoke soothingly to her and soon coaxed her out.

"Inside," Aulic ordered impatiently, grasping the wolf-girl's arm to propel her forward.

Cassie detested the lack of respect he always showed towards the wolf-people, and her anger flared. "I'm taking this one, Aulic," she said, and she pushed his hand away.

"Now, then, Miss Cassie," he growled. He had never liked the child and at times found it hard to hide the fact.

"It's lucky that she's come at this time," Cassie

answered. "I was looking for a maid for myself, you know. *A personal* one."

Aulic scowled.

"Come on," said Cassie gently to Tara. "Follow me." She swept past Aulic, hiding her grin behind her haughtiness, pulling Tara along with her.

Tara took a while to get used to being inside a building, especially one so dark and sprawling, full of closed doors and receding passages.

They sat side by side, shyly at first, on Cassie's bed, and Tara told of her impetuous leap on to the cart in the wood, and of the feeling that somehow she did not quite belong to her pack. Under Cassie's careful probing, she revealed something of what it was like to be a young wolf, learning to blend in with the pack, to use foliage as camouflage, to track down game, to listen for signs of danger...

In turn, Cassie described her life in the Mansion with her father, Lord Tancred, and her twin brother Keiron. Her father, she said, was a mage and scholar, far more interested in things found in books and scrolls or maps of the heavens than in the life around him, but she and her brother loved him, for all his eccentricities. They spent their day studying, reading stories, playing shuttlecock, roaming in the woods nearby when the weather wasn't too bad, and talking to their father in the evening when he took his mind off his books.

Tara noticed that Cassie made no mention of her mother. Not being close to her own parents – wolf-people merge into the pack from an early age – she did not hesitate to ask about her.

"I don't know," Cassie mumbled, shaking her head slightly and looking away. "Father won't tell us."

"Why not?"

She shrugged. "He likes mysteries, I suppose." She smiled ironically, then took a deep breath. "No, that's not it. I think something happened to my mother when Keiron and I were infants. Father says she didn't die, exactly, she just, well, changed." The subject confused her and she found it hard to talk about.

"Like we do, you mean?" Tara said brightly. "Change from wolf into human and back again."

Cassie considered this. "Perhaps that's it. Although, if she can change back into human, why have we never seen her?" She fell silent.

The wolf-girl was fascinated by the tall mirror in Cassie's bedroom. She shied away from her reflection at first, then touched it in puzzlement – it was so much clearer than anything she had seen in water. Growing bolder, she tried to reach her image by looking behind the mirror. Her bewilderment, her wonder, delighted Cassie.

For the rest of the day Tara tried on Cassie's clothes, shrieking and laughing at the sight of herself in them; and then they wandered around the Mansion. But Cassie didn't at first introduce her to Keiron and her father: she was too pleased to have the wolf-girl all to herself.

"I'm so glad I caught sight of you behind that water-butt," Cassie said. "If I hadn't, you'd be down in the wolf-quarters with all the others and I might never have noticed you."

Tara smiled. "I feel ashamed of the fear I felt," she said.

"Well, you've nothing to fear now. And don't take any notice of Aulic. He likes to bully the wolf-people, but if he ever tries it with you, you just let me know."

"Thank you," Tara murmured. She slipped her arm through Cassie's.

"You won't mind being separated from the other wolf-people," Cassie asked, "to be up here with me?"

There was a glint of happiness in Tara's slanted eyes which Cassie could not mistake. "I shall love it here," the wolf-girl said.

She slept on a large cushion at the foot of Cassie's bed, curling up as if she was still a wolf, and sometimes Cassie would hear her yelping softly in her sleep, as if she was still running with the pack.

While Cassie had been making friends with Tara, Keiron had been in his room, sprawled against the base of his bed with his bare feet toasting before the fire. There was a large, old leather-bound book on his lap, full of his favourite stories written out in a careful calligraphy. He wondered vaguely what was keeping his sister; probably chatting with the new wolf-people, he thought, turning the page. He knew he should be helping to show the new wolf-people around the Mansion, but he could not tear himself away from the book and the fire.

He was reading one of the many legends about the Golden Armour. There was a picture of the Armour opposite the story, lying on a slab of rock in the temple vault, its golden gloves folded on its breastplate, a glow emanating from it in the mysterious gloom. Such pictures always stirred something deep, nervous and dangerous in his imagination, as if for a moment he had caught a glimpse of another reality far more exciting than his own.

One story he particularly liked told of an exiled king who landed on Temple Island with his grown-up son and found the Golden Armour in the ruins of the temple. The goddess Citatha asked him to take the Helmet, the Shield, the Spurs and the Sword and place one of each on the four main islands. "They hold my magic," she said. "Whoever can unlock it will transform these islands into a paradise, where I may rule again."

The king did as she asked, keeping the Helmet for North Island where he settled. He built a castle on the northernmost tip of the island, and waited for the Helmet to work its magic. But nothing happened!

Keiron wondered what came first, the story or the castle. There was a teasing quality about these stories which unsettled him: were they history or fantasy?

He turned the page and came across a picture of the king's son, a tall, handsome youth with blazing, hypnotic eyes. This prince quarrelled with his father, he read, and fled to East Island. There, he found hideous monsters which he hypnotized and mastered. He built a great dome to house the Golden Shield; but, like his father with the Helmet, he could not work its magic: Keiron delighted in the numerous attempts the prince made, each more original than the last, to unlock the Shield's secret.

Keiron closed the book with a satisfying thump.

He felt a movement in his hair.

Well, Will, he said telepathically, *what did you think of that one?*

In his long, uncombed, flaxen-coloured hair, Will, Keiron's little wooden manikin, stretched and yawned. He was no taller than Keiron's hand.

About a year ago, Keiron had carved him out of a piece of willow he had found in the forest. He had "seen" the shape of the wooden boy in the bark, in the contours of its twigs and knots. Will – as Keiron promptly, if rather unimaginatively, called him – emerged from the wood almost as if the knife was simply peeling back layers of wood fibre to reveal him already there.

Cassie had soon got interested in the manikin. "He looks so real, in a funny sort of way," she observed, studying his face, his glossy green eyes. "If only..."

Then a miraculous thing happened.

She stroked Will, concentrating hard on his inertness, hardly aware of what she was doing; and when she felt the sap agitate within him, she wished that he was alive. Suddenly, he wriggled in her hands. She was so startled she shrieked and dropped him. Will fell to the floor, sat up, looked up at them in bewilderment, then scratched his head and grinned.

When she was still a small child, Cassie had discovered that she could heal little creatures that seemed sick: she'd stroke them and feel some sort of energy flow into them from her fingers; and suddenly, they'd scamper or fly away as right as rain. She did not understand why she had this power, but it was all of a piece with other inexplicable things in nature, and the twins had got used to it.

But she had never brought alive something hand-made before, and she did not know what to make of it.

Now there were three of them. For quite some time, Cassie found it hard to get used to the idea that her brother had someone else to turn to now, someone ever closer to hand than herself; and she was always a little cool and mocking towards Will.

Keiron had a gift too – not such a powerful one, but inexplicable nevertheless. From an early age he had learnt that he could "speak" to things in his head. Wood, stone, pottery, weave, sand, water, mud, whatever – they all had a voice in his head and would answer his questions if they had a mind to. It proved quite a useful gift, too: for instance, if he mislaid things, he could ask where they were, or if he got lost he could ask his way home. Occasionally, too, if he was bored, he might ask something old to tell him its life story, which could be quite amusing.

It was because of this gift that he and Will were able to talk to each other telepathically, and that was the best use he put it to, by a long way.

Well, what did you think of that story? Good, wasn't it? Do you think the Golden Armour really exists? said Will.

Of course I do! And one day, Will – I'll tell you this and no one else – I'm going to find it.

It was meant to be an idle boast, but somehow it came out differently. Like a prophecy echoing from another time. And Keiron shivered.

* * *

Cassie brought Tara in to meet her brother. They smiled and nodded at each other shyly. He was fascinated by the wolf-girl's slanting, almond-shaped amber eyes, by the way she put her head to one side on hearing faint sounds far away in the building, by how her nose twitched too as she picked up currents of scent he had no inkling of. She was beautiful, too, in a dark, wild, woody kind of way; her skin was very white and unblemished, her hands were long and thin.

Keiron was a little startled at the closeness that had sprung up between the two girls; normally, since they only spent a month with the wolf-people, there was never enough time to make friends with them. And she was so young. But he felt happy for his sister: he had sensed lately that there were times when she needed a friend besides himself.

For a while Tara was tongue-tied in the boy's presence. She could see the close resemblance between him and his sister – the same texture and colour of hair, the same bright, searching look in their eyes, the same unconscious gestures of friendliness – but it was the differences that struck her. While Cassie was like the dark reflections on a pool in a wood, he reflected the wavering light, his thoughts passing like fish just under the surface: that was her initial impression.

"And this is Will," said Cassie, snatching the inquisitive manikin from Keiron's hair. "He can only speak to Keiron, no one else. Hold him, if you like."

Being both from the forest, Tara and the manikin had their own instinctive language; it was made up of signs and touches, and the twins watched delighted as Tara and Will got to know each other. He ran over her, peered into her ears, got her long silver-brown hair in tangles, slid down her arms and eventually settled on to her lap.

"Here, Cass," said Keiron, picking up the leather-bound book, "I found a new picture of the Golden Helmet."

They all stared at the full-page illustration. Something hypnotic seemed to emanate from it. Tara shivered and turned away, as if a cold draught had passed over her. Will sat on the edge of the page and slowly shook his head.

"It's very handsome," said Cassie. "But the darkness in that visor scares me a bit. I don't know why. Like there should be eyes there, not emptiness."

"I know," said Keiron. "I'd love to put it on, wouldn't you? Oh, Cass, we should look for the Golden Helmet. All the stories say it's here, on North Island. Don't you think?"

Cassie's face brightened, and she opened her mouth to speak.

"I can hear the wolves howling in the wood," Tara interrupted, lifting her head. A look of pain came into her eyes and she turned away.

Cassie felt for Tara's hand. It was cold.

"You don't wish you were with them, do you? You *could* go back if you wish. I could talk to Aulic about it."

Tara shook her head.

"Come on, then," said Keiron, trying to cheer them up. "Let's settle down and hear another story."

CHAPTER 2

The wind changed direction and swept in from the swelling seas off North Island. It moaned around the thick-walled Mansion where Cassie and Keiron sat either side of a log fire that cracked and glowed. It was a week later and Cassie was reading aloud another story from the leather-bound book. The wind fidgeted at the mullion windows and hummed down the chimney; it curled around turrets and seeped through keyholes and cracks. The twins took no notice of it: it had sung and and howled in their ears, like a giant baby, since their first glance into the world. They would have sat up and listened only if it had grown silent.

Cassie looked up from her book. "I wonder how the pieces of Armour found their way to the different islands."

Keiron's eyes lit up and he said eagerly, "There's a story a bit further on about that. An exiled king just gave the pieces away. He thought that that was what Citatha wanted. Well, if a stranger knocked on our door and said, 'Here's a golden Helmet for you; it has hidden magic,' you'd be grateful, wouldn't you?"

The imaginary Helmet hovered before his eyes. He wondered what magical thing would happen if he put it on.

Cassie turned the page. "But the goddess couldn't have known what humans were really like, could she," she observed. "I suppose, when the islands were just one, like a paradise, everyone was good. She probably never saw their darker side."

She yawned. "You read now," she said, her eyes suddenly feeling heavy. . .

As soon as Keiron touched the dry, crackling paper and saw the faded pictures, the figure of the goddess Citatha stepped into his mind. He had been told about her with his nursery rhymes and fairy tales; she was an essential part of his inner world. Sometimes he dreamt of her, and of the Golden Armour lying half-complete in the ruined temple.

He began to read aloud a new story. It told of the coming of a great horde of nightmarish monsters from East Island. They had been brought over by the wicked son of the exiled king, or so the story said. Cassie loved the descriptions of the great, dragon-like salamanders, and she shivered at the thought of the giant, leathery birds flapping menacingly overhead. They settled in and around what was now called the Ice Castle on the northernmost tip of the island.

"I'd like to see those stone monsters," said Keiron. All around the Ice Castle were stone monsters, so real as to seem petrified in another time, in a great freeze. They were terrifying in their ugliness.

But Cassie's imagination was roaming elsewhere. "There's another story here which says that whoever puts on the Golden Helmet will get what they wish for. Have you read it yet?"

He shook his head. "What would you wish for?"

Cassie looked into the fire and her face took on a dreamy look. "I would wish that this island be like it once was. All the islands. One big paradise again, just like it was before the Great Volcano. Think of that! No more cold winds, no more black skies and sleet, no more frozen north, no more horrible, long, dark winters. We'd have beautiful plants and flowers and butterflies and endless, warm sunshine. . ."

Her words penetrated Will's sleepy, wooden skull. *It makes me weep to think about it*, he sighed.

What does?

How things used to be before the Volcano.

So you believe all that?

Of course! Will sounded almost indignant.

And about the monsters from East Island?

Yes!

How do you know? Aren't they just stories?

Trees have long memories.

You couldn't remember yesterday.

Huh! I was a seed once, remember. And a seed carries the memory of all its ancestors, right back to the goddess's time. So there!

Keiron pictured the Golden Helmet turning slowly like a planet in space. "If the Helmet was real. . ."

"Father thinks it's real."

"So does Will. And if it is. . ."

"We should search for it."

"Yes! All the stories say it's on this island. What if it really is?"

Cassie saw how brightly his eyes shone, how eager he looked, and she smiled to herself. It was always so easy to get him fired up.

She got up, her head still full of visions of sunlit landscapes, and leant out of the casement window. Great, grey, rolling clouds were casting dark, moving shadows over the land. The distant ridge looked like a bar of darkness and the dark copse to the right bent in the wind. Ravens strutted on the battlements to her left, and to her right two white owls turned their large, amber eyes in her direction, murmuring in their snowy throats.

She turned back inside. "There's no sign of the hunt. They should be back by now."

"You're thinking of Tara, aren't you? She'll be all right."

Cassie shrugged. "It's her first hunt as a human. She didn't show any fear, but when I touched her I could feel her trembling."

Keiron stood with hands outstretched at the fire. "Let's go and see what Father is doing," he said. "He hasn't been near us all day."

"I think there's something on his mind," Cassie said. "When I looked in on him this morning, he was scribbling furiously at some chart. He didn't even notice me. And he was muttering, you know the way he does when his brain is racing ahead of itself."

They pushed open the carved oak door of Lord Tancred's study and they found him drawing imaginary lines in the air between planets and stars in a great model of the universe. Made of wood, it showed stars, moons and planets that revolved around one another at the turn of a handle. His thin, nervous face was twitching, and his brooding eyes were flecked with a strange gleam. Beckoning them to be seated on a huge sofa, where they were in danger of being submerged in a mountain of tapestried cushions, he seized a parchment on which was drawn an astrological chart, and cried out, "Look at this! Such a conjunction has never been seen before!" He stared at it disbelievingly, shaking his greying locks.

"What is it, Father?" Cassie asked. She was used to his fits of wild excitement, but this one seemed more intense.

"Catastrophes. And hideous conflicts. Change everywhere! There hasn't been such an alignment since..." He threw up his hands in despair.

Handing the twins the chart, he said, "You see where the red planet is on the chart?" he said. They found the planet. "Well, the same planet is here." He pointed to a small, angry looking planet among many in the model. "Now watch how all the moons and planets configure with it." He turned the handle, the globes revolved and circled, until he reached a certain point. "This is *now*."

The twins looked puzzled.

"Here," said their father impatiently. "Take a pencil and join up the planets and moons and sun on your chart. Start with the red planet and move anti-clockwise."

Intrigued by this, Keiron grabbed a pencil and began to trace a line on the chart from one heavenly body to another. Cassie was content to sit back and watch him, and she was the first to observe what the outline began to describe. In the far north of the island was a frozen sculpture of a huge salamander – a kind of bearded dragon – a look of agony and despair on its ancient face. She knew it well from the many pictures of it and from stories that had been written about it. As Keiron finished the drawing of it, she had the sensation that the great salamander was moving, stirring in the depths of its centuries-long slumber.

"That's amazing," Keiron murmured. "What does it mean?"

Their father took the chart and studied the drawing. "It means we must be on our guard. Vigilant in a way we have never been before." They had never seen him so worried. Scared, almost.

"But on guard against what?" Keiron asked.

"The stars do not tell us that," said his father, shaking his head. "They are never specific."

What use are they, then? Will suddenly murmured close to Keiron's ear.

Lord Tancred reminded them of catastrophes in the island's history – the minor earthquake, the melting of an iceberg, floods, epidemics – and set beside each the astrological charts of the time, drawn up by his ancestors. The twins listened with awe; their father's beard trembled, his eyes darted nervously, his voice rose and fell.

They were so deep in these lurid and colourful histories, they failed to hear the arrival of the hunt, back from a five-day trip in the forests in search of deer meat and furs. There came a loud rap on the door, which was opened by a wolf-man servant. "The hunt has returned," he announced.

Tancred barely registered the message. Cassie thought anxiously of Tara, and she rose from the cushions to find the wolf-girl. But Keiron held her back. There in the doorway, brushing the servant aside, was Aulic, still in the thick, black bearskin coat.

Aulic was the master of all the Mansion's servants. As a young man, he had wormed his way into the confidence of Lord Tancred's aging parents, and had been in charge of the great, labyrinthine house ever since. He made sure that everything ran smoothly. He was indispensable, and Lord Tancred knew his worth, even if he didn't much like him.

Aulic gave a quick, curt bow to his master, and an even briefer one to the children. Cassie stiffened. She saw the exhilaration in his eye and felt a new kind of energy in his bent and wizened, stiff little body.

"Sire," he said. "I bring interesting news."

"Well, go on," said Tancred. He said to himself, *It is starting already. I can see it in his eyes.*

"We travelled right out to the northern peninsula, for we heard from some trappers that a herd of deer had moved that way. And there we found tracks, of horses and sledges, that seemed to be heading for the great Ice Castle on the furthest tip." He paused and wiped his mouth. "Then we were hailed by a lone horseman from the castle."

"From the castle?" Tancred murmured. The place had been uninhabited for as long as anyone could remember, except occasionally by bands of wandering trappers.

"The horseman asked many questions about you, Lord Tancred."

"Who was he?"

"He would not say."

Keiron felt Will stirring in his hand. *I know who he is. And his coming will freeze the sap in every tree*, the manikin murmured to itself.

Not now, Will.

"Would not say? Did you not demand it of him?"

"I tried, my lord, but he was too haughty."

"Did he say where he was from?"

"He mentioned East Island."

"Ah," said Lord Tancred, his brow creasing. "East Island? What is he doing here?"

"He did not say, but he said to tell you that he wishes you no harm. He has come to stay a while in the Castle. He says it once belonged to a distant ancestor of his."

"Ancestor!" Tancred turned to the window, deep in thought. "Then I think I know who he might claim to be. And I do not like it." He glanced back at his charts. The twins watched him anxiously. Aulic stared at his feet, the very slightest smile playing on his lips.

"How many people has he got with him?"

"We did not see, my lord. But judging by the tracks, we would guess no more than twenty. He mentioned his aunt; the rest I judge to be servants and hangers-on. He is no threat."

Huh!

Shhh, Will.

"You were not invited into the castle?"

Aulic shifted uncomfortably and loosened his coat a little. "We were, my lord, and I for one would have gone... But..."

"You were frightened!" Cassie jumped in, accusingly.

Aulic drew himself up. "No, dear girl, not I," he contested. "But the rest of the party were. It is a truly frightening place. Many of them had never been that far north before; they did not know of the hideous and petrified creatures that loom everywhere in the trees. Have you seen the stone monsters, my lord? They look as if they'd come alive at any moment." Aulic allowed himself a little shudder. "And besides, it is perpetually icy up there. It is not a place any of us wanted to linger in."

"I see," said Tancred. "Tell me more about this mysterious visitor."

"He's about twenty, tall, with a thick mane of dark hair, a compexion almost like the ice itself, and with a pride in his bearing that … that…" Aulic was lost for words. "Magnificent, in his way," he murmured.

"Keep an eye on him, Aulic," Tancred ordered. "We can't have a stranger coming in and claiming part of the island as his own, however remote and inhospitable it is."

Aulic bowed, and sensing his audience was over, he slipped out.

"Well," said Tancred. "It's just possible we have a princely visitor amongst us."

"Princely?" Keiron echoed, staring at his father.

"If I am not mistaken, this man is the son of the Queen of East Island. I wonder why he has come here?"

"Shall we meet him?" Cassie wondered. Aulic's description of the dark prince had stirred her; she could already imagine his bright, disdainful eyes and the shock of unruly black hair.

"Why not? If it is him, we must find out why he has come. Perhaps we might arrange a hunting trip for ourselves. It's time you two went on one that lasted for more than a day. And we may as well travel north as anywhere."

"You mean, to the Ice Castle? To see the petrified monsters?" Keiron exclaimed excitedly. His father nodded, his mind elsewhere.

Cassie disentangled herself from the mountain of cushions that had built up around her, and unexpectedly put her arms around her father. She felt he was troubled by this news, and by all the portents he had discovered in the heavens, and she wanted to comfort him. But this time he did not unbend, and she let go of him, unsatisfied.

CHAPTER 3

Cassie took an oil-lamp and set off in search of Tara. She was a little puzzled that the wolf-girl had not come directly to her room as soon as her duties were over. She went along gloomy corridors, treading on rush-matting, ignoring the shadows flickering all around her and the scuttle of vermin behind the wainscot. Here the wind moaned and growled like a discontented dog, pawing the windows and rattling the frames. She trod carefully down a stone spiral staircase to a passage that led to the servants' quarters. As she approached it, the pungent smell of the wolf-people grew in strength. It wasn't unpleasant, but it was one she could never quite get used to.

She shivered; the cold down here clung like an invisible mist.

She wondered about the thieves who, generations ago, had stolen so many of their wolf-skins. Who were they and why had they done so cruel a thing? They must have known how much it would cost the wolf-people.

The terrible theft had happened on a night when the

wolf-people had slipped out of their skins and were being their hidden human selves. They jumped and swam in the river, climbed trees, rolled down hills and wrestled with each other, celebrating all those things they could not do so well as wolves.

But their high spirits turned to horror when they discovered the theft of their pelts. They hunted in vain for them.

Since then, a tradition had grown up that the ones without skins worked as servants in the mansion where they could be sure of keeping warm and could better learn the ways of being human. Each month a new batch of wolf-people came to the Mansion, and thus none of them was their naked human self for more than that period.

But the problem of the missing pelts persisted from one generation to another. And it *was* a problem, not just at the practical level. The wolf-people as a species felt compromised, sullied, damaged, and dishonoured by the theft; it was a permanent wound in their side. They would never be happy until the skins had been found, yet few of them now thought there was much possibility of that.

And for some it was worse. If, by some cruel misfortune, they became mortally wounded or ill, they suffered terrible agonies, for it was considered a great disgrace to die in their human form.

Cassie, pondering all of this, pushed open the door of the servants' quarters. It was a long, low, subterranean room, with pallets down one side where the wolf-people slept, tables, cupboards, crockery, clothes on the other side; a narrow passageway ran down the middle. She was met with many friendly greetings as she carried her lamp through the lightless hall – for the wolf-people retained their faculty for seeing in the dark – and she was directed to Tara at the furthest end.

The girl was asleep.

"She is exhausted, poor thing," the wolf-woman who was looking after her whispered to Cassie. "We came across another pack near the great forest, and all the cubs surrounded her, wanting to know what the Mansion was like. It was hard for her, for many of them were her friends. Then, when we tracked down the quarry, she hid her sight from the blood and flesh."

Cassie saw scratches and streaks of mud on Tara's skin.

"She fell off her horse into brambles and tumbled into a stony river. Being human has confused her; but she'll learn."

"I'll look after her now," said Cassie.

She roused the sleeping girl and had her carried back to her bedroom. She washed the wolf-girl's body of its mud and placed her in her own bed.

"Well, was the hunt as bad as you thought it would be?" Cassie asked.

"Worse, I should think! I've been on hunts before, but I've never been in the thick of it. And I felt so clumsy in my human form: it's not made for hunting, is it?"

"You'll soon get used to it," Cassie laughed. Then she added, "I wouldn't mind being a wolf myself for a while, just to see what it is like. The world full of smells, currents of them everywhere, ears that pick up noises we never hear as humans, and a body that can streak through the undergrowth..."

Tara slipped out of bed and looked at herself in the lamplit mirror. She tucked her hair behind her ears. "I'm getting to like being human, though," she said, almost in spite of herself.

"Good," said Cassie.

"But is it?" She sighed.

"Why, what's the matter?"

"I've always enjoyed watching the hunt before. So exciting. But not today. The sight of pain and blood and horrible wounds... It sickened me. I even let a hare go free because I couldn't bring myself to kill it. Is that because I'm becoming more human than wolf?"

"Perhaps."

"But it's happening too quickly." Tara's bright, slanted eyes were full of doubt.

"Don't worry," said Cassie. "Make the most of it while you can. Here, let me brush your hair."

Tara shook her head. "I like doing this," she said.

"Yes, and every time you brush, your tongue comes out, as if you'd rather lick your hair," Cassie said teasingly.

Tara, laughing, handed the brush to Cassie.

"While I'm brushing," said Cassie, "you can tell me about this visitor in the Ice Castle that Aulic is so excited about. Did you see him?"

"Oh, yes. He smelt of strange creatures, not ones we have here."

"What did he look like?"

"A great, black raven, with eyes sharper than a sliver of stone, and skin like snow. His hair was like water eddying in a dark stream. I have seen no human like him. And when he looked at me..." She closed her eyes.

Cassie grasped the wolf-girl's shoulders. "Tell me," she demanded softly.

"His eyes fixed on me, bored into me, like beams of light in a mist. All the strength went out of me. As if he was drawing it out. I felt I would do anything he would ask me to, even against my will. He saw the wolf in me, and I obeyed."

A few days later, the twins and their father wrapped themselves up in furs against the vindictive wind, and climbed on to horses outside the Mansion. Despite the vicious weather, the twins could hardly contain their excitement; they had been awake since dawn, ready to leave before anyone else was up and about. Accompanying them were many wolf-people on horses, on sledges and carts, with food and tents, bows and arrows, spears, slings and staves. Two held falcons on their wrists. They were going hunting for sport.

Tara sat, well wrapped up, in a cart under a deerskin. Cassie waved enthusiastically to her. Will poked his head out of a hole in Keiron's woollen hat, his tiny green eyes, like glossy seeds, missing nothing.

For several days they rode into the heart of the island and beyond, trying to steer a course so that the buffeting, biting wind was always behind them. From time to time they stopped in sheltered places. Lord Tancred showed his children the arts of hunting, winging birds, felling rabbits, spearing fish, even how to chase off a lumbering bear. They were allowed to hold a falcon on their wrist and were shown how to release it. The excitement of it all, and the approval of their father, banished what scruples they had against killing for sport.

At night they stayed in villages and trappers' huts, anywhere they could find. The children huddled together under mountains of fur, trying to get warm. One night hailstones the size of eggs pounded unceasingly on the roof of a house made of logs, the noise keeping them awake until dawn. Another night the wind was so strong, they feared the village lodge-house in which they were staying would be lifted from the ground and hurled against the hillside. As they travelled north, the air grew colder and colder, the ground and the gaunt trees glittered with frost, and each time they spoke clouds of breath issued from their mouths.

About noon on the seventh day, they came in sight of the Ice Castle, a dark and craggy silhouette cut against the grey of the shifting clouds. Here the wind, as it swept in off the sea, had a sharp, rasping sound, broken by hisses and whines as it buffeted itself against rocks and statues and stunted trees.

All about them, among the leaning trees, were the likenesses of hideous creatures, as if cut into dark rock, and glistening with frost. Cassie stared at a crumpled heap, half obscured by rotting leaves, and she could just make out the twisted form of a dragon-like bird, its savage beak broken, its leathery wings splayed and twisted. Will pointed out to Keiron a giant lizard with a jagged edge, like chipped teeth, along its back, and a leer in its frozen face. Tara huddled with the other wolf-people, talking in their own yelping language, glancing fearfully at the petrified creatures all around them. Only Lord Tancred looked at them with any scientific interest.

The hunting party stood on a little hill, and looked at the castle. The wind fidgeted like a hostile guard dog around them.

"I've only ever been inside it once, when I was a boy," said Tancred. "And it was so cold, so sinister, I couldn't get out of it quick enough. We must not linger here."

A horseman appeared at the great double doors of the castle, a sharp silhouette etched against the grey wood. They paused and watched him as he galloped through the trees and frozen monsters, on a winding path towards them. They waited like statues themselves, while he cantered up the hill and swerved to a halt, his horse whinnying at the jerk of the rein.

With his thick black hair and dead-white skin, he was undoubtedly the one that Aulic had spoken of. He wore furs on his shoulders and thick, woven leggings, yet for all that he had a fiery kind of elegance.

"Lord Tancred, if I am not mistaken," said the intruder. There was no sign that he was out of breath. "I have been expecting you. I hope you will pause a while in my castle, that we may talk."

His dark eyes settled on each of them in turn as he spoke. The power that Tara had spoken of, the power of drawing out their resistance, was felt by each of them in differing degrees.

Yes, thought Cassie, watching the wind snatch at

his thick black hair, he is all that Tara said he was, and worse.

A sudden thought struck Keiron. Maybe the Golden Helmet is somewhere deep and dark in this terrifying castle, perhaps hidden there by an ancestor of this man, now lost in the folds of time. (He had been thinking a lot about the Helmet lately.) Perhaps it's covered in cobwebs and looks like the cocoon of a giant moth, or perhaps...

Your mind's wandering, said Will.

I might be right!

Don't you think he's searched that castle already, from top to bottom?

What, him? How do you know he wants to find the Helmet too?

Oh, I know, said Will. *Why else has he come here? I can see it in his eyes: they remind me of those shiny beetles that get under the bark of trees and eat and eat until there's nothing left but a hollow, a ghost tree. You'll see I'm right.*

"And who are you?" Tancred demanded.

"I am Prince Badrur, son to the Queen of East Island."

CHAPTER 4

The tall, gaunt grey castle was covered in a network of thick, frosty branches. As the party approached it, the horses grew nervous, tossing up their heads, whinnying and jerky. Tara burrowed into the furs on the sledge, her blood afire as the poisonous hypnotism in the prince's eyes crept through her being. Keiron shuddered at the sight of a twisted dragon-like creature, both its wings crushed and its snout bent, its eyes closed in agony. *I'm glad it's dead*, he murmured to Will who was shivering in his breast pocket. *Sleeping*, Will corrected ominously.

Cassie kept her eyes fixed on the handsome horseman who was leading them into the castle. Every fibre of her being said resist him, not least because she knew how suspicious her father was of him. And yet, why should she fear him? What power had he got over them? He had looked at her with, she thought, a hint of admiration at the haughty way she had stared back at him, resisting the magnetic power of his eyes.

A ragged group of men pushed open the ancient wooden doors of the castle and the party swept into the courtyard. In the sudden dimness among the looming brickwork, sparks from the horses' hooves flared defiantly.

The prince led them up wooden outer stairs to a large, shadowy room. A fire flared in a cavernous fireplace; huge, mouldering tapestries, indistinct with hunting scenes, hung down one wall, with rusty swords, spears and shields between the narrow windows on the opposite wall. Standing by a long trestle table was an old woman. She wore a thick robe of some dark, fine material that had once been red but was now a faded brown, and in her hair which hung in loose, wiry grey strands down to her shoulders, there was a battered-looking tiara.

"This is my aunt, Angharer," Badrur announced. "She will make you welcome."

Where Badrur was all pride and contempt, his aunt was all obsequiousness. "I am so, so glad to see you," she declared. "Here, come by the fire and warm yourselves..." She fussed about them nervously. Cassie noticed that she darted glances at Badrur from time to time, as if to make sure of his approval.

"My aunt was kind enough to accompany me to this wild and frost-begotten place," he said to Tancred. "Have you ever been to East Island?"

"Once."

"Then you will remember how hot it is, how dry. How everything burns up."

Tancred nodded.

"I don't miss the sunshine," Angharer put in, smiling.

Of course she does, Will murmured, deep in Keiron's breast pocket. *She's like a bulb in winter, wondering if she'll ever flower again.*

Prince Badrur motioned to a man standing by the doorway and ordered some refreshment. They all settled around the long table.

"Despite the cold, I find myself curiously at home here," he said. He held out his hand. "Look at that," he said softly. They all stared at the hand. "White, is it not?"

Solemnly, they all nodded.

"The blazing sun had no effect on it. Even my aunt is tanned, but not me. 'Ice runs in your veins' my mother says, but I did not really know what she meant until she told me about this castle."

"Where's Tara?" Cassie suddenly demanded, her voice loud and strangely cracked, so that she began, uncharacteristically, to blush as all eyes swivelled round to her.

"Who's Tara?" Badrur enquired.

"My wolf-girl friend, my maidservant."

"She stayed on the cart, I think," said Keiron.

She was terrified, said Will.

"Do you want her to come in?" Badrur asked softly. His fingers touched her hand. Cold, burning ice. Sharply, she pulled her hand away and shook her head.

"Not if she's happy where she is," she said, trying to control the strange fluctuations in her voice.

The manservant brought in a tray of stone cups, with handles in the form of snakes, and thick slices of bread covered with a strange but delicious-smelling paste. The children took theirs suspiciously but were surprised at how good both the drink and the spread tasted. *You'd be even more surprised if you knew what it was*, said Will with a chuckle. *Then don't tell me*, said Keiron.

"And what did your mother tell you about this castle?" Tancred asked, swilling the liquid around in his cup.

"Oh, its history, its legends. I'm particularly interested in an old story Angharer used to tell me. A prince of East Island came with a great horde of monsters – the ones you see frozen around this castle – in search of the Golden Helmet. You may know of this story?" Tancred nodded.

"He already had the Shield, but he wanted more."

"Did he find the Helmet?" Keiron asked eagerly.

"He did, but it did not do him much good. He died in the snow."

Angharer smiled fondly at this memory. "It's all true. It's history," she declared; and Badrur nodded in agreement.

"My mother tells me I'm descended from that first prince." He stared around at them, his eyes glowing hypnotically.

"And you believe her?" Tancred asked.

"I do. My mother is not one to make up stories. Besides, I feel that he and I are one. We have so much in common. He must have loved the cold to come here, even if it eventually killed him. I am at home in the cold, too. I hardly feel it. I do not shiver in the wind or feel pain when I put my hand on an icy rock. I love the frost, the snow, the bare trees. Don't you think it's all so beautiful?"

In the silence that followed this, a log in the fire shifted and a little shower of fiery ashes briefly flared in the dank air.

Tancred stirred under the weight of Badrur's gaze. He had come here to say something. What was it? Ah, yes: "But of course, you do realize that this castle is in my domain, despite what you claim regarding your ancestry."

"This castle once belonged to the first prince. I believe I am descended from him." He looked at Tancred challengingly.

Tancred looked alarmed. "If you can prove your connection..."

"How can I do that?" he shrugged. "But I believe I have a claim to this place." He rose from the table. "You and I have much to discuss, Lord Tancred," he said with a formality that made Tancred feel apprehensive. "I suggest that Angharer takes the children on a tour of the castle. It might amuse them."

"Oh, good," said Keiron, getting up at once.

Cassie thought her father looked worried. "I'd rather stay..." she began, but faltered when Badrur's gaze fell on her.

"You go, Cassie," Tancred said softly. "There is nothing to fear."

The twins followed Angharer down some stone stairs to the ground floor, barely listening to her prattle, forming impressions of their own. Will clung to Keiron's hair, grimly determined to miss nothing, noting how little grew in this blighted place, no pot plants, no shrubs in the courtyard, only the gnarled tendrils of a tenacious ivy here and there on the walls and moss on the ledges.

Keiron glanced about him, all the time seeing places

where the Golden Helmet might, just might, be hidden: behind a loose brick or under a flagstone perhaps, or inside one of the monsters, or even disguised – until his head was filled with too many possibilities.

"Look at your hand!" he said to his sister a moment later.

Badrur's icy finger-touch had left five marks on her skin, like burns. She rubbed at them, furiously humiliated. *How dare he!* she kept saying to herself.

"Do not worry, child," Angharer said, taking the girl's reluctant hand. "Badrur leaves his mark on everyone; but this one will not last."

They moved through dim chambers; there were signs here and there of certain rooms inhabited by the prince's servants and hangers-on, but most of the rooms were cold, damp, disused. On the upper floors, looming in shadowy corners, or set in stone alcoves, were petrified creatures, like macabre statuary. A huge, winged bird stretched over one wall; fat wasp- and spider-like creatures were arranged along a mantelpiece; scorpions sat like rusty fire-irons in the grate; squat reptiles of every shape sat on window-sills.

Angharer stumbled over an armadillo-like creature with a fan of broken blades around its neck and shuddered. "I quite happily told Badrur all about these hideous things when he was a boy. He couldn't have enough of them. But I never thought that I would have to live with them one day, even if they are dead."

Cassie crouched down beside the lizard and touched its dusty head.

"Don't bring it alive, Sis," Keiron said, half-laughing.

"Why do you say that?" Angharer asked.

"Oh, he's just being silly," Cassie murmured hastily. She looked up at the old woman. "The legend says the creatures came from *your* island. Have you got any there now?"

Angharer cackled. "We have scorpion-guards, half-people, half-scorpions," she said. "And some rather dreadful lizard-people. But not monsters like these, I'm glad to say." She laughed again, and then grew pensive. "Come on, I want to show you something curious, something we've only just dis-covered. Perhaps you can shed some light on it."

They followed the stiff old woman up a winding staircase into a large round chamber. It was empty except for what looked like dried animal skins hanging from the ceiling. They walked among them wonderingly. Angharer reached up and touched one. "They have lost their suppleness," she said. "They're too dry, too stiff, to be of any use. I don't know why. Furs usually remain supple, but something has got into these and petrified them. I cut one down when I first discovered them and tried to soak it in water, thinking to soften it, but it simply disintegrated. Should I cut them down and dispose of them? I can't say that I feel easy about them."

Oh, never do that, said Will. *It'd be worse than cutting down trees.*

"Never do that," Keiron echoed instinctively.

Angharer looked at him surprised. "You know what they are for?" she asked.

"Haven't a clue," said Keiron cheerfully. "Probably some old dame in times past who liked to dress up in fur. Who knows?"

A look of disdain passed across Angharer's face; this was not the time for levity.

Cassie, meanwhile, had wandered to the back of the room and had found a skin that hung lower than the others. She reached out and began to stroke it. Under her fingers the fur suddenly became supple and glossy – it came alive. She stroked it dreamily, wondering what Tara's pelt of fur must be like, before she realized the change the dried fur had undergone. Fascinated, she ran her hand all over it, turning it into something fresh and glossy; it even took on the smell of wolf-people.

Angharer was suddenly at her side. "How strange," she murmured, watching Cassie intently.

Cassie snapped out of her dreamlike state. "Yes, look," she said, "this one is still fresh."

Keiron touched it too. He caught Cassie's eye and understood.

"But I can't think how that can be," Angharer murmured.

"I expect someone has been out hunting and killed a young wolf," said Keiron. "They shouldn't do that here, you know. The wolves are half-people. You should tell them."

Angharer barely took in what he was saying. She had a feeling that something vital was happening here but just beyond her vision. She moved to the door, thinking to get advice from her nephew. "Look, I must leave you for a minute."

They listened to the old woman's footsteps die away. The oppressive silence of the castle stole over them.

What do you make of all this, Will? The castle and everything? Prince Badrur?

Nothing will grow here, said Will. *But life is dormant everywhere. I feel it.*

Isn't that good?

No, said Will abruptly, calling this exchange to an end. There were some things he couldn't put into words, only half-understanding them himself.

Cassie reached up and tugged at the wolf-skin that she had brought alive. "I want to take this with us." She tugged as hard as she could but it would not give. "Keiron, help me."

They were both so intent on getting it down, they failed to hear Angharer's sudden return.

"Please don't do that," she commanded. Her voice had a hard edge and they both let go of the skin in surprise. "You must leave this room now." They followed her out reluctantly. "Forgive me for leaving you just then," she said, consciously softening her voice. "Let us continue the tour."

She eventually took them up to the roof. The wind hummed a strange, angry tune through the battlements and turrets, rising and falling, buffeting them as they leaned against the old stonework. The view stretched over the trees and beyond into snowy wastes one side, and across the heaving, metallic sea on the other side. Black gulls hovered and cried above the din of the wind.

"This is a sad and bitter place," Angharer said. She had murmured it to herself, but the wind caught it.

"Why did you come here, then?" Cassie asked.

"Because of him. Why do you think?" But she said it without bitterness. "He's always dreamt of coming here. He's quite convinced he's descended from the first son, the one in the story."

"Are these the same monsters?" Cassie asked, pointing towards the hideous stone statues in the trees below.

"Yes, so the legend says. The island froze and all perished, including the first son and these monsters."

"And after that, the Helmet disappeared," Keiron said to himself.

"Do you always do as he says?" Cassie asked.

Angharer shook her head. "It's not like that."

"What's it like, then?" Cassie persisted.

The wind snatched at Angharer's straggly grey hair and made her eyes smart; but for the next few minutes she looked almost dignified. "I brought Prince Badrur up, you see. I was his wet-nurse, his governess, yes, even his mother. *She* had no time for him. She said he was too cold, like a changeling. But I loved him."

"And you still do," Cassie observed softly. From the first moment she had seen Aunt Angherer, something told Cassie to be wary of her, but at this moment she only felt tenderness.

"I did not have any children myself," Angharer confided. "He still finds it useful to have me by his side and I can't refuse him. I never could refuse him anything." A wry smile played on her lips.

"Why did he come here, then? Really?" asked Keiron, anxious to exploit the old woman's sudden confidence. But his voice cut through her memories and brought her back to the present. "He's always dreamed of coming here, claiming it as his own. That's the reason. No other."

Cassie swept her gaze over the bleak landscape.

Suddenly, she had a dream-like vision. It only lasted for a few seconds, but in that time she saw the Golden Helmet radiating light and warmth over the whole island; she saw the land transformed into a paradise of green, of birdsong and glistening water, of young creatures emerging from their burrows... She was almost overwhelmed by it and closed her eyes tightly to calm herself.

"Cass?" he whispered, nudging her anxiously.

She seized Keiron's sleeve and said urgently, "We must find the Golden Helmet, Keiron, we must..."

He caught the excitement in her eyes and understood.

They rejoined Lord Tancred and Badrur in the hall. The prince was leaning against the stone mantelpiece, apparently deep in thought.

"Extraordinary man. Extraordinary mind," Tancred muttered to his daughter as he rose to go. "Like something out of a legend himself."

Cassie could tell by the tone of his voice that the prince had gained her father's confidence. She was troubled by that. She felt Badrur's gaze settle on her again and she returned it defiantly. Yes, he was handsome, with his white skin, his thick black hair, his irresistible eyes, but she sensed the ice in his heart. Surely her wise old father could sense that too?

Keiron edged up to Badrur. "Earlier you mentioned the Golden Helmet?" he said.

Badrur stared at the boy, surprised. "What about it?"

"I just wondered – " He faltered, aware that perhaps he might be overstepping the mark.

"Whether it might be hidden somewhere in this castle?"

Keiron nodded. He felt as if the fierce eyes of the prince were laying his heart bare.

Badrur smiled ironically. "I've searched everywhere for it, and so have my men," he said. "If it is here, it's well hidden. What's your interest in it?"

"Oh, nothing," said Keiron feebly. "I've just read about it. So you think it's real, then?"

At that Badrur laughed out loud and Keiron felt foolish.

"Farewell, then, Prince Badrur," Lord Tancred said, mounting his horse in the courtyard. "We shall meet again soon."

The cart passed through the castle gates, and the driver cracked the whip, anxious to leave that place as quickly as any of them.

Tancred looked back at the gates closing behind them. "The prince is coming to stay with us," he announced.

"With us?" said Keiron, surprised.

"Better to have him on our side, than against," said Tancred. "He has unusual powers, that young man. He may be of use to us."

Cassie felt Tara tremble at this news.

On the battlements Prince Badrur watched the sledge and the horses disappear into the snowy wastes. He was tossing a stone in his hands. An unsuspecting gull glided past. With deadly accuracy, the stone flew from his hand and struck the bird in its plumy breast. He smiled faintly as it plummeted in a whirl of feathers to the ground.

When Angharer showed him the live pelt in the room where the dried skins hung, and told him how Cassie had stroked it, he questioned his aunt closely.

That night she began to pack his belongings for a prolonged visit to the Mansion.

CHAPTER 5

News of the imminent arrival of the strange prince disturbed everyone in the Mansion. The wolf-people talked about him endlessly. In particular, they said that he could hypnotize animals and make them do cruel, humiliating things. There were stories of him making bears grovel at his feet, snow-foxes dance for him on their hind legs, birds dive-bomb sheets of lake-ice, knocking themselves senseless – all for his passing amusement. They spoke of him as an ice-man, carved from a glacier, with frost for skin and melted icicles in his veins.

Tara brought all these stories to the twins. It made Cassie suppress lingering admiration for his looks, and Keiron hate him; but neither could still a sense of excitement and apprehension at his coming. The sleepy old Mansion was coming alive, jittery and mysterious, and this suited their growing desire for something different, something *new*, to liven up their lives.

Even Tancred, preoccupied in a renewed study of books about the Golden Armour, picked up the twins' excitement and, at meal times, tried ineffectually to dampen down their anticipation. "He won't want to be bothered with children, and he'll scarcely notice the wolf-people. Keep out of his way, all of you. He is coming here to join me in my researches into the Golden Armour."

The twins glanced at each other. "He wants to find the Helmet too, doesn't he?"

"Of course he does. He is as anxious to find it as I am. I'm sure, if he and I put our heads together..." Lord Tancred leaned forward, his hand trembling slightly. "And I have something to show him," he said mysteriously, "something I've been working on for a long time, which..." He paused.

"What is it, Father?" Cassie asked eagerly.

Tancred smiled teasingly. "You will see in good time." He wouldn't reveal more, despite their attempts to wheedle it out of him.

Aulic was almost beside himself with anticipation. He took it upon himself to supervise personally the preparation of Badrur's room. He had it cleared, washed and swept out, an almost unheard of event in any of the Mansion's living-quarters where the marks and dust of time became part of the fabric. The best bed, chairs, rugs, curtains, armour for the walls and tapestries, were plundered from other rooms and arranged so tastefully the room itself became a sort of spectacle to be viewed with awe and discussed in whispers. Keiron patted the little man on the shoulder in genuine enthusiasm, but Cassie frowned disapprovingly. She did not like the way they were making Badrur so welcome; or was she simply jealous that he, and not she, was thought worthy of such a room?

"But he is a prince," Aulic said insinuatingly to her, underlining her inferior status – at least in his eyes.

The twins watched from their window as the lone horseman paused on the ridge, not much more than a small black speck, then galloped the last stretch down the slope, through the trees and on to the wide track that led to the Mansion's gates. Until he arrived, the whole house seemed in a state of suspended animation. Now, as he flung aside his reins and strode past the obsequious Aulic, the spell was broken, the place came alive. Wolf-people pressed themselves against the wall as he passed, their metaphorical hackles rising. Aulic hurried after him, attempting to direct him, but Badrur seemed to know instinctively where to go. He met Tancred, Cassie and Keiron in the great hall.

After polite and nervous welcomes they sat in a half-circle around the fire. Aulic hovered about them irritatingly, directing the wolf-servants to bring wine and cakes.

Prince Badrur began by being charm itself. He described his journey with such lively detail, making a joke of tricky encounters with hostile trappers and fierce hailstorms, of tracks that halted abruptly at cliff edges and precarious bridges over roaring ravines, of a wind so strong that at times he felt almost airborne on his horse, and did it in a way so free of that menacing, sapping, hypnotic gaze, that despite their feelings for him they were all charmed. Even Cassie warmed to him. Only Tara, hiding in the shadows, kept a look out for the hidden dangers that she sensed around her mistress.

Later that afternoon, the twins were sent by their father to see how the prince was settling in. They found his room in an uproar. Aulic, pale-faced and sweating, was standing by Badrur's chair, apologizing to him in one breath, shouting blustering directions at the wolf-servants with the next. Cassie guessed at once what had happened and, clapping her hands with glee, she laughed.

"I'm sure Aulic meant well," Badrur explained, obviously enjoying the servant's discomfort, "but really I can't abide all this stuff, it has no character. My own furnishings have just arrived. And besides, this room is far too poky. I need space, I need to spread my wings. I practically had a whole palace to myself when I was young."

"We had no instructions, you see," Aulic tried to explain. "And this has always been the guest room."

"Never mind, Aulic," Cassie said with a delighted wave of her hand. "You will have to find Prince Badrur a bigger room."

That night, after supper, Prince Badrur showed the twins and their father what he had made of his new room. It was lit by strangely smelling lamps. "Oil from a peculiar cactus on East Island," he said. "It burns for ever." There was no bed, simply a mound of furs and cushions. On a low table was an array of elaborate pipes and hookahs, with bowls of crushed powders and dried herbs.

"These help me to think, sleep, dream, have visions," he explained to Keiron who was examining the pipes with interest. "You must try some sometime."

Keiron saw the gleam in Badrur's eye and shook his head. "My dreams are bad enough already," he explained, half-serious.

Above the fireplace hung a huge tapestry. A salamander writhed exaltedly in a frame of fire. The picture was repeated in burnished shields that gleamed above the fireplace. Badrur said softly to Cassie, whose eyes had been drawn to it, "For me it is the symbol of East Island."

"It looks rather cruel. Don't lizards like water?"

"That one does," he chuckled. "But everything burns up on East Island, sooner or later."

"Except you," she said, looking at him critically.

He smiled. "You are like my mother," he murmured. "Always judging by appearances."

That stung her. "And what about you?"

"What about me?"

"It is said you are cruel to animals. Is it true?"

"I have a hypnotic power over all creatures. It is my gift."

"Then you should use it to help them, not torment them."

He laughed at the way her eyes blazed, her cheeks flared. "And what is your gift, Cassie? If you're anyone special, you should have one." He said it teasingly, but the way he said it – as if he already knew what her gift was – unnerved her, and she turned away.

He joined her father and they were soon deep in conversation.

"What was that about, Cassie?" Keiron whispered.

Cassie didn't answer. "Look at the way he's getting round Father," she said in disgust. "I don't like it,

Keiron. I don't trust him. What has he really come for?"

"To find the Helmet," Keiron answered. "I'm sure of it."

Their father and Prince Badrur were closeted in Tancred's study for the next few days, and the twins were not allowed to disturb them. They were only to discover what the two men were doing when Tancred summoned his children to the great hall one morning for "the ultimate demonstration of all my studies" as he grandly put it to them.

Lord Tancred was in the great hall at first light, assisted by Aulic, but no one else was allowed in until word was sent mid-morning.

As soon as Tara brought word, Cassie and Keiron raced downstairs. They burst in to find a great cauldron simmering above a fire and their father standing by the table in a long gown. On the table were a number of books, as well as powders, herbs, and other twisted and dried ingredients the origins of which were unguessed.

When Badrur strode in, Tancred wiped his brow and said, "We may begin. Let me explain what I'm about to attempt. I've spent my life studying documents about the Golden Armour, looking for a pattern. And I think at last I have found one. A sequence of potions, a chain of chants: these I have put together. And out of it will come a vision. Maybe that vision will speak to us."

Keiron felt Will wriggle up his shirt and sit astride his collar. *I never thought he'd get this far*, said Will.

Well, you shouldn't be so sceptical.

And your father shouldn't be so trusting.
Be quiet.
There won't be any quiet after this.
Shhh!

Lord Tancred picked up a book and began to chant some verses. Every so often he paused and, taking something from the table, he threw it into the pot. Sometimes there was a hiss, sometimes a cloud of steam, sometimes only silence. Finally, the table was bare except for the books and some drawings of the Golden Armour.

"Now we are ready. You can all take part in this."

He picked up four drawings. "Cassie, you have the Helmet. Prince Badrur, you the Shield. Keiron, the Spurs for you. And Aulic, the Sword. I want each of you at my signal to put your drawing into the cauldron. You first, Cassie."

Cassie stepped forward wonderingly. Did her father really know what he was doing, or had he got lost in some romantic idea? She did not want him to look a fool in front of Badrur; and what might he be giving away? She let go of the drawing of the Helmet and on contact with the steaming liquid, it curled up. Tancred chanted incantations from a book.

Each in turn did the same.

Badrur threw his in carelessly, as if he found all this a bit childish. In the past few days he had assisted Tancred in his preparations, and had gained the lord's trust, but he could not quite believe all this ceremony would get them anywhere.

"Now, the final piece," said Tancred. He picked up a magnificent engraving of the Golden Armour, cut from a huge bound volume, and approached the cauldron. Keiron noticed his hand was shaking.

Tancred intoned something in a tongue none of them recognized, and then he tossed the engraving into the cauldron.

There was a loud hiss. A yellow cloud of steam filled the room. A golden light emanated from the cauldron. It grew stronger, having the intensity of fire but without the heat. Those watching stepped back and shielded their eyes, wondering what power Tancred had unleashed.

The yellow steam seemed to draw back into itself and form a solid shape. It became the outline of a body, hard and shiny: a helmet, a visor, chain-mail, gleaming leggings, spurs, a great shield and a sword. There dazzling before them was a vision of the Golden Armour. It hovered above the cauldron like a powerful and luminescent ghost.

For several minutes none of them moved. The twins' hearts were thumping hard. Will shielded his eyes, peeping out from time to time, thinking, *Once you've let it out. . .*

Lord Tancred viewed it with absolute wonder. He had conjured parts of it before, but never the whole; and there was an aura about it, a presence, which made previous manifestations pale and fleeting in comparison.

Every fibre of Badrur's being now was ringing with the thought, *I'm on to it at last.*

Suddenly the vision of the armour began to rotate slowly.

Keiron rose and stood by his sister. She felt for his hand.

The dark hollows of the Armour's eyes and the slit for the mouth, gave it something of a human aspect, and they both began to feel that a voice might issue from it. They held their breath, waiting for its message.

But Badrur was impatient for something to happen. He rose too. Suddenly, in a fit of impatience, he reached out to grasp the Armour. His hand simply passed through it. The Golden Armour wavered. A look of fury passed over his face and he reached out, grasping, again and again.

"Don't do that," Tancred shouted in distress.

But it was already too late. The Golden Armour wavered so much it began to disintegrate. The golden solidity shivered back into mist.

Badrur turned away in disgust at himself. Tancred looked on helplessly, distressed at this abrupt and destructive end to what should have been a magnificent triumph.

The mist hung in a cloud and slowly cleared.

They gathered around the table in silence. The twins looked at their father in awe and sorrow. He closed the books and absently brushed up stray herbs and seeds.

"That was impressive," said Badrur at last, looking at his host with grudging admiration. "I don't know how you did it, but... "

"Our father's a magician," Keiron interrupted proudly.

But like all magicians he's only playing at the edge of the dark forest, Will observed gloomily.

"It was beautiful, wasn't it?" said Cassie, boldly addressing Badrur. "I bet you weren't expecting that!

My father's very powerful. It is a pity you couldn't have just watched it."

Badrur nodded. "Lord Tancred," he said. "Forgive my little lapse. I was so moved, I..." He gestured with his hands as if to say, I'm sure you understand.

Tancred sighed. "Well," he said, staring at the last wisps of mist in the air, "this is confirmation, as if we needed it, that the Golden Armour is more than just a legend. It has powerful magic."

"Especially when complete, eh?" said Badrur.

"I believe each individual piece has its own power," said Tancred. "But put together..." He shrugged, as if to say, it's beyond human understanding.

"The Helmet looked almost frightening, didn't it," Cassie said.

"I wonder what happens if you put it on," said Keiron.

"I wish I knew that," said his father.

"Then let us search for it!" Badrur interrupted impatiently. "Such gold does not perish. It's eternal. Somewhere, that Helmet still exists. When was the last time anyone searched for it?"

"We have always looked for it. At least, our ancestors have."

"Precisely! Everyone gave up looking for it ages ago. But this vision of yours, this ghost you have conjured of the Golden Armour, don't you see it as a sign?"

"You mean," said Cassie, suddenly catching Badrur's excitement, "the goddess Citatha might be working through us, through my father."

"Yes," said Tancred, catching hold of the idea. "All the portents are there. It would explain why the astrological charts are full of strange predictions and conflicting influences. This could be the time."

Badrur rose and stood before Tancred. "I pledge myself to help you find the Golden Helmet. It will be my mission from now on. Perhaps that is why I have always felt the pull of this island, perhaps that's why I came."

Tancred's eyes glittered. "Your help in this matter will be most welcome," he said formally.

The twins looked at their father in dismay. Why did he trust Badrur?

He's too blinded by the glitter of the Armour, Will murmured.

"Then let us begin at once," said Badrur.

The two men, with Aulic at their heels, left the twins in the great hall.

The children peered into the cauldron. There was nothing there now but a brackish liquid choked with paper, twigs and plants.

"I can't believe what we saw come out of this, can you?" said Cassie.

"But we did see it," said Keiron. "We know what the Helmet looks like now. You said you wanted to find it. Do you still want to?"

"Of course," said Cassie. "But not with him."

He's like the cuckoo, said Will.

Cuckoo?

The bird that doesn't belong. The bird that pushes out the weaker birds.

He might help us find the Helmet.

And then?

Keiron had no answer to that.

"I can't help thinking," said Cassie as they left the hall "that the Armour was about to speak."

"I got that impression too," said Keiron. "I wonder what it would have said to us?"

CHAPTER 6

Wolf-people can scent danger in the wind. Tara felt subtle currents of it in the Mansion and she knew its source. For herself, she was afraid that if she ever fell into Badrur's clutches she would become his plaything; and she continued to fear for Cassie too. She kept watch on Badrur's movements. As long as she evaded his energy-sapping gaze she thought she would be safe; and she enlisted the help of the wolf-people, who were as uneasy about him as she was.

So Badrur was watched closely – the hours he spent puffing on his pipes and hookahs, the strange mutterings and cries in his sleep, the restless wanderings through the Mansion at all hours, the wild gallops in the surrounding countryside when the horses were whipped to exhaustion, the frenzied, erratic searches for the Helmet in every nook and cranny of the building, the long hours closeted with Lord Tancred poring over books, maps and documents relating to the Golden Armour – all were noted.

The wolf-people hoped that he would give up his fruitless search for the Helmet, or at least leave the Mansion on a wider search for it. But Tara began to suspect that the prince's plans were changing. Why, for instance, did he suddenly make friends with Aulic? What were they planning together in Badrur's room? Why was Aulic seen carrying a hookah to Lord Tancred's study? And was it wise for the lord to take up the habit, filling his study with a strange acrid smell and a lingering miasma that made her feel sick?

The twins found themselves largely barred from their father's presence. The vision of the Golden Armour, the hovering presence of the prince, the sense of urgency brought on by the portents he had revealed, the renewed desire to track down the Helmet, had whipped up in him a storm of mental excitement, in which his children had no place. He spent night and day poring over maps of the island, linking obscure hints and symbols in books and legends to places on the map, drawing strange diagrams, always having something to discuss with Badrur when the prince returned from one of his searches. He slept and ate little. He became obsessed.

Cassie was suspicious of the pungent powders and ground herbs Tara said her father had taken to smoking: she wanted to know more about them. One morning, with Keiron by her side, she knocked bodly on his study door, knowing well that he had forbidden them to visit him without permission.

They were shocked to see how his appearance had changed. His eyes were red-rimmed and watery, his face drawn and white, his movements jerky; but worse than that was his manner: the abruptness, the twitch of his head, the rattling nervous cough. He looked at them as through a mist of words and symbols and intractable mysteries, hardly seeing them.

"Father!" Cassie cried.

"You look – dreadful!" Keiron said at the same time.

He did not respond to their concern. His eyes blinked rapidly as if to clear a film over them. In desperation, Keiron told him of their fears about Badrur, while Cassie tried to warn him against whatever he was smoking in the hookah. It was blurted out and incoherent and it only seemed to rile him.

He rose unsteadily and glowered at them. The words seemed to gather in his mouth before he spat them out. "You accuse a noble prince," he said, "and bring disrespect on this house. It is disgraceful!"

"But Father..." Cassie began, astonished to be spoken to by him in this way.

"No! He has told me of your insolence. I do not want any more of it. Isn't he dedicating himself to helping me in my life's work? How dare you!"

The twins stood open-mouthed as he harangued them. Never had he treated them like this; and as they stared at the spittle around his lips, at the trembling of his waxy cheeks, at his livid eyes, they both thought: this is not the father I know, this is someone else. It pained them inexpressibly, and they slunk out at his abrupt dismissal with their hearts beating in fear and dismay.

"Tara was right," Cassie announced when they got back to her room. "Badrur has put something in that hookah of his which has turned Father's mind. He's not himself."

Glumly, they sat on Cassie's bed, wondering what to do. Tara hovered uncertainly nearby, listening with her acute hearing for the approach of him whom she had come to hate more than anyone.

A day or two after this, the twins were playing shuttlecock in a small courtyard – it was more a battle against the wind than each other – when Tara scurried out to them. "Badrur is leaving the Mansion for good," she shouted excitedly. "He says he's going to scour every bit of the island until he's found the Helmet."

Keiron looked at Cassie. "Will he find it? He won't give it to us if he does."

"He *mustn't* find it," Cassie said, shaking her head in dread of the prospect. "If he puts it on and it gives him magical power…"

The island would freeze up and we'd all perish, said Will.

Keiron repeated Will's words. The twins stared at each other, imagining the prospect with such vividness, they shivered with cold.

"We must find it first," Cassie declared.

"But how?" Keiron wondered. He hadn't exactly been idle in that respect since they had returned from the Ice Castle, and, like Badrur, he'd come to the conclusion that the Helmet wasn't in the Mansion.

"Somehow," said Cassie. "If only for Father's sake."

With Prince Badrur's departure, the heart gradually went out of Lord Tancred's search for the key to the whereabouts of the Golden Armour. He had moved from maps to following several textual trails; he had been working at the same time on diagrams hidden in well-known paintings of the founding myths; at night, in the sleepless hours, he had been trying to crack cryptograms. Each had yielded something tantalizing which excited him for a while and spurred him on. But in the end he felt that all he had achieved was like a vast tangle of wool, made of many threads which only a man of infinite patience could untangle.

And he had to admit even to himself that he wasn't feeling too well, either. There were vague pains in his stomach, sudden weaknesses in his limbs when he rose from his desk, and blinding headaches that struck without warning and forced him to lie still on his bed; truly, he had been overdoing it. The only relief he found from this came through the hookah that Badrur had given him, and from the ground-up mix of unidentifiable ingredients that Badrur had supplied with it: something that soothed his pains, and set him floating in a woozy dream-world that threw up flashing visions. Aulic kept him supplied with it and cleaned the hookah each day, making sure that it was ready for him to smoke whenever he needed it.

Sometimes, when he felt his mind was on the edge of some appalling abyss where all sorts of monsters lurked, their eyes gleaming in the dark, he invoked the memory of the only woman he had ever loved, the mother of the twins. She, glowing silver light, was a touchstone and comfort; but even she was indistinct now, more like a shape in a mist, and he had to reach out blindly to catch her hand.

One night he awoke suddenly and sat up, his mind

blazing with an image of the Helmet. Though he was extraordinarily weak, he felt himself almost being pulled from his bed by some invisible force. In his long, crumpled nightrobe, and with only a flickering oil-lamp to guide his faltering footsteps, he made his way trance-like through the Mansion, down a long connecting passage and into the Chapel.

He shuddered in the gloom of the place, the glass rattling softly in the window, the sills and panes catching the fitful moonlight. What was he doing here? He stumbled forward and with shaking hand put the oil-lamp down on the flagstones. Before him stretched the polished black altar stone: everything else in the Chapel had been rebuilt or replaced many times over, but this stone was thought to be the original.

With a sense of extreme fatigue, Tancred lowered himself on to the dark slab and stretched out like an effigy, his hands clasped on his chest. The cold of the stone struck into his bones.

He had no idea why he was doing this. He felt impelled; he had no choice.

There passed before his eyes a vision. Of his children, standing in a pool of light, surrounded by the fierce eyes, the drooling teeth, the slashing claws, the gyrating necks of monsters roused from some paralysing sleep. Of Prince Badrur raising the Helmet above his head and crying victory. Of some dark infantile force creeping blindly towards them, and of Tara the wolf-girl standing alone against it. His teeth chattered and his body trembled...

Darkness stole over his mind. His body grew colder.

As Lord Tancred slipped into a dangerous kind of unconsciousness, there came another visitor to the Chapel that night. Aulic, prey to a conflict between conscience and ambition, had got into the habit of rising at odd hours of the night to check on his master. Half of Aulic hoped to find him sleeping peacefully, the other half wished the effects of the hookah would be more decisive and send his master into madness. He debated with himself all the time about whose side he should be on, barely noticing how much he muttered out loud as he went about his business.

The empty bed had seemed ominous – and horribly promising. A couple of sleepy wolf-men were roused to search for Tancred. Aulic wandered about, searching half-heartedly, until word was brought that there was a light flickering in the Chapel. Wolf-people were not allowed in the Chapel, so Aulic went down the chilly passage alone. He peered into the cavernous gloom of the place and saw Lord Tancred stretched out on the altar like a corpse. He shuddered, thinking he was in the presence of death. But then a faint sound of breathing could be heard in the brief lulls between the gusts of wind curling about the building. He crept forward and held his lamp over the gaunt white face of his master. It looked peaceful and for a moment Aulic's conscience overwhelmed him. He knelt down and asked for forgiveness, shaking Tancred ineffectually as he poured out his pitiful excuses for what he had done. Tancred did not respond, and when Aulic ran out of words, the silence was like a rebuff.

He rose abruptly, and in a sharp change of mood

he sneered at the body, and said, "Well, let nature take its course, then."

He ran to the doors and slammed them shut behind him. For a moment he leaned against them, breathing heavily, then he fished from a pouch hanging from his belt a giant bunch of keys. Selecting the most ancient one, he inserted it into the lock with trembling fingers even as his conscience bid him not to, and locked the Chapel doors.

As the cold seeped into Tancred's body his heart beat slower and slower, his breathing grew fainter. In the chill of the hour before dawn he might have died. But other forces just as deep were activated that night.

A clear spell in the night sky brought the full force of the moon's rays into the Chapel. Out of the silvery moonlight there formed a familiar shape. It shook itself free of the light, and into the darkness stepped a sleek, feline creature, larger than a domestic cat, all the fibres of its fur glowing with silver. Now the Chapel itself seemed moonlit, even in the darkest corners. Rats melted away, spiders scurried into crevices, even the wind's howl softened.

Silver Cat prowled softly round the body of Lord Tancred. An afterglow remained behind her as she moved, so that Tancred's body was soon inside a wavering circle of light. Then she leapt on to the altar, up beside his head. She placed a paw on his forehead. Tancred's breathing became steadier and deeper. His pulse increased in strength.

Silver Cat stayed like that, motionless, until the moon lowered itself into the dark forest outside and sunlight crept over the sills.

Who was Silver Cat? No one knew, not even Tancred, the one she loved best. She appeared in secret, to protect the few that meant everything to her, and she seemed to be made of moonlight.

Tara the wolf-girl woke in the night too. Her acute sense of hearing told her that there were strange movements in the Mansion, but for a long time she refused to uncurl herself and investigate.

She too saw Tancred's empty bed. She ran silently through the building, pausing to look here and there, but because it was out of bounds to wolf-people, she did not think to look in the Chapel. Then, through a window, she heard Aulic in the courtyard below shouting for wolf-servants. Peering out of the window, she saw him ordering them to load up a cart. "Where is he going at such an hour?" Tara wondered. "It's like a demon has got into him." She watched as the great double gates creaked open and the cart and horses clattered out. Aulic himself cracked the whip.

Tara woke Cassie and told her of her father's disappearance and of Aulic's abrupt departure. They hurried to Tancred's room, rousing Keiron on the way. Apart from the usual disorder, there was nothing there to indicate where their father might be.

"He wouldn't have left the Mansion, surely?" Cassie wondered. "Not in his state."

"And not without telling us," Keiron added.

"Perhaps Aulic got word of where he is and went after him?" said Tara. But the propect of that was hardly a comfort.

Aulic is like a rotten branch, said Will. *He'll soon fall off.*

Then what shall we do?

Use your gift.

My gift?

You must have sensed it. It's not just a game.

You mean ... how things talk to me?

Do you have another gift, then?

But what do I ask now?

Will sighed in exasperation. *Ask where he is. What else?*

Keiron was fired with excitement. He looked round wildly, then seized the hookah that was on his father's desk. He concentrated his mind on it, then said to it telepathically, *You who have done so much damage to his mind, tell me where he has gone.*

There was a voice in his head that came from the hookah. *I saw him leave, that is all.*

"Come on," said Keiron to the others, both of whom were looking at him in surprise. "You're not the only one with a gift, Cassie. Remember?"

In the passage he spoke to the rug.

Yes, his feet trod here last night.

A window-sill said, *He rested his hand against me.* A dusty tapestry said, *He looked like someone sleep-walking.* The stair-carpet said, *His tread was heavy. I thought he might fall.*

By this means they eventually reached the entrance to the Chapel passageway.

The doors were still locked.

Keiron peered through the keyhole. He could just see the edge of the altar and – was that his father's foot?

Lock, he said. *Who turned the key?*

The keyholder. Who else?

And is my father in there?

He lies sleeping.

They banged on the door but, worryingly, he did not stir.

"We must get this door open at once," said Keiron.

"Aulic has the keys. Would he have taken them with him?"

They turned over Aulic's room. They found quantities of their father's hookah mixture, but no keys.

Just as they were about to despair, Will said tentatively, *Let me try. I'm small enough to get into that lock. Maybe I can do something in there.*

Back at the Chapel doors, Keiron carefully placed Will at the lip of the lock and Will wriggled inside it. Being a huge, old lock there was room enough for him in there. He sat for a long time in the rust-smelling darkness working out the mechanism, oblivious to Keiron's impatient whispers and questions.

I need a wire, he said at last.

Tara fetched some and Keiron fed it into the lock. Will attached it to the tooth of a cog and then said, *Pull*. Keiron pulled, there was a grating sound, and the lock opened.

Lord Tancred had a deathly pallor and felt very cold, but on taking his pulse Cassie whispered, "He's still alive."

The twins kept vigil by their father's bedside. He drifted in and out of consciousness, smiling at them when awake, his eyelids flickering when he was asleep. It was with difficulty that they got him to eat anything, and he remained weak. It seemed as if half of him was far away, in some other realm. Occasionally, he would ask for his hookah, but when that was denied him, he became querulous and then fell into a silent despair.

"I want my father back," Cassie wailed a few days into their vigil.

"There's no life in him any more," said Keiron, equally fretful.

Something happened to him in that Chapel, said Will.
What?

I cannot tell that. Something frightening. Then something that made him happy. He's poised between the two. In limbo. It reminds me of that time between winter and spring when you're not quite sure if it is safe to open your buds.

I don't understand you.

Then you should find someone who does. Your father will survive bodily, but his mind is at stake here. His roots.

Who can help us?

When he told Cassie and Tara what Will had said, Tara's face lit up. "When any wolf-people are sick, we go to Magda, the medicine woman. She lives in a cave in the woods with another pack. She has saved wolves that were troubled and other animals that have been wild with some pain of the mind. My own father was once troubled by the thought that to be human was better than to be wolf, and she gave him some potion which cured him of it. It is a common complaint with us. She might help your father."

In one of their father's lucid moments, they told him of their decision to find Magda and to ask her for a potion to cure his mind. It took him a while to grasp what they were talking about, and then a piercing thought lit up his eyes with pain and he cried out, "It's not her medicine I want. No. The Helmet! Prince Badrur must not find it! We are all dead if he does. *Find the Helmet. Or we die...*" He closed his eyes and sank back on his pillow, exhausted.

The twins instructed some trusted wolf-people to tend Lord Tancred, and then with a last farewell to him, which he hardly understood, they mounted their horses and galloped down the track from the Mansion into the windswept island. It was the first time they had been out braving the dangers of the island without the protection of their father.

CHAPTER 7

They travelled towards the heart of the island, sometimes galloping on the crest of the wind, sometimes – as the wind veered erratically from one direction to another – bent over the horses' manes, clinging on precariously. A thunderstorm of sleet and hailstones overtook them towards evening and, drenched to the bone, they found shelter in a friendly hamlet where the people lived in huts raised up on stout stilts.

The storm rumbled all night and hail pummelled the huts with a never-ending roar, but the children managed to sleep through some of it.

They emerged next morning to a sea of mud through which their horses picked their way with difficulty. Then, about midday, when they were sheltering under a clump of trees against a squally wind, a posse of horse-riders cantered past.

Tara quivered. "I think that was Prince Badrur," she said.

"He's still searching for the Helmet." Keiron reminded them. "That's what we should be doing, too. If it's not in the Mansion, it must be out here somewhere."

"We *must* find it first," Cassie said. "I wonder what Father meant when he said we'd all die if Badrur got to it first."

"Just his mind wandering. We must get that medicine."

The second night was spent in a hut used by trappers and hunters. Many such huts dotted the island; they usually contained animal skins, damp and mildewed, and logs for a fire. The ashes in the centre of this one were still warm and the children were able to make a welcome blaze.

Early next morning Tara woke the twins. "We have visitors," she said. "Outside."

They stumbled blinking into the light, to be greeted by a ring of wolf-people sitting in silence in front of the hut. Normally, wolf-people showed signs of friendliness, wagging their tails like dogs, or holding up a paw; or else they sped past with barely a nod of their heads. This wary silence was unusual.

"Talk to them, Tara," said Cassie. "Surely they know who we are?"

Tara crouched on all fours and bared her teeth: at that moment, Keiron thought, you could hardly tell whether she was human or wolf, and he watched her, fascinated. She yapped softly. The wolves tipped their heads, as if listening; some softly pawed the ground or whined. Tara's yapping rose a little, then she grew confused. One of the wolves answered, then another, until several were yapping at her at once.

"They do not want us here," she said to the twins.

"Why not?"

"Because Prince Badrur was here yesterday."

"So?"

"These wolf-people guard Magda. He went to her yesterday and threatened her."

"Threatened her?" said Cassie. "Why?"

"They say he wanted her magic to help him find the Helmet. She refused."

"Good for her," said Keiron.

"Have you told them why *we* must see her?"

Tara nodded. "They are reluctant to let any more humans near her. She is much agitated."

"Then you must go alone to her," said Cassie, "and convince her. Our father's life hangs in the balance: she won't refuse us when she is sure of that."

Tara proposed this to the wolves. They broke their circle and surrounded her, sniffing her, nudging her with their noses, licking her, until they were sure that she was not an impostor. Then she mounted her horse, waved to the twins and galloped away, the wolves rippling like a sea of silver around her.

The twins spent the morning huddled by the fire. For the first time in their lives, they felt alone and unprotected, their future uncertain.

Will took the opportunity to scamper off amongst the trees. He climbed bark and roots and swung on tendrils. He washed himself in a leaf-cup of dew and burrowed playful tunnels through fallen leaves. He chased a tiny, furry creature with a stick, but fled when confronted with a black spider twice his size, its eyes glaring on stalks. Then he settled at the foot of a venerable old tree and just listened to the delicious and multifarious noises of the wood.

Tara galloped back just after midday, her eyes

glowing, her body more alert and alive than it had been for a long time. She had good news. "I had hardly opened my mouth, and she understood," Tara said, speaking of Magda. "She says you must come at once."

The wind, behind them, assisted their passage, and they sped along a well-trodden track almost airborne, their horses' hooves rhythmic on the soft earth. Wolves joined them as they neared the complex of caves where Magda, the medicine woman, lived, until the earth all around them seemed to be seething with undulating fur.

She met them at the entrance of the caves. She towered above them, her smoky-grey, yellowing hair bushing out, full of twigs and leaves, around her gaunt leathery face and down to her waist. She wore layers of thickly woven material tied with a fantastic net of twines, and from her belt hung leather pouches full of secret ingredients. Her feet were swathed in fur-lined boots and she stood upon a carpet of flax.

The twins were mesmerized by her eyes: they were crystal clear and blue as a kingfisher's wing; in fact, they were so at variance with the homespun chaos of her garments, they seemed to belong to someone else, someone not quite of this world.

"Your father has always been aloof," she said, in a surprisingly soft, almost gentle voice. "He was even so as a boy. Always his head in the clouds." She smiled briefly. "But I knew that one day his offspring would come begging for his life. You have left it rather late."

Plucking up courage to speak, Cassie said, "But will you be able to help him?"

"There are greater forces ranged against him than you could possibly know," she sighed, shaking her head. "But I can find an antidote for the poison he's imbibed. Those who made it are but novices in the art. Come, I have already begun preparing it, based on what your good Tara has told me."

They followed Magda into the cave. The flax carpet gave way to furs and cushions. From the ceiling hung bunches of drying plants and herbs, and on the walls were drawings of animals, stars, symbols and strange diagrams. At the back, haunches of smoked meat hung and, lower down, cauldrons of various sizes simmered over a fire, giving off pungent odours of wood, herbs, earth and bones.

Magda stirred one of the cauldrons with a stick. "It will take some time for this to be ready, so let us talk." She motioned them to sit on a mound of furs and, ladling a liquid from another cauldron into wooden bowls, she bade them drink. It had a strong taste, unpleasant at first, but curiously warming and reviving.

I wish I could drink that, said Will, peering enviously into the dark green liquid. *It's the forest's nectar. Only she knows how to distil it.* The little wooden manikin looked about him with wonder. This place, that drew all its substance from nature, and this woman, who seemed to him like a tree incarnate, full of age and mystery and secret sap, was the nearest Will would ever get to a temple.

As the drink took its effect, the twins grew in confidence. Cassie put down her bowl and asked, "What did Prince Badrur want with you?"

"Huh!" she barked, smiling sardonically. "He has become obsessed with the Helmet. And like all men who become obsessed, he will trample on any thing to get what he wants. He thinks I have the second sight and can see where it is. Well, even if he was right, he'd be the last person I would tell."

"We are looking for the Helmet too," said Keiron eagerly.

"I am aware of that," Magda said, stirring her cauldron. "The wolf-people tell me all I need to know."

"Then, you will help us?" Cassie asked.

"Please," said Keiron. "We don't want it for ourselves."

Magda nodded thoughtfully and turned to Cassie. "Does he speak the truth?"

"We want it for our father," the girl answered. "But for much more than that. If the legends about it are true."

"True? In what way?"

"That somehow, the Golden Helmet can turn this island into a paradise again. Like it was in Citatha's time."

The goddess's name had a galvanizing effect on Magda. She raised her arms above them, her eyes glittering sharply.

"Sit against the dark wall," she said imperiously.

They moved obediently to where she indicated. She sat motionless in front of them and stared hard. "There is a silver light, like a tough thread, all around your auras," she murmured. "It is the light of the goddess Citatha. You are powerfully protected. And yet I cannot believe it is because of your father. He is a mage of sorts, but his power is weak, he can only summon visions and dreams: no, this comes from your mother."

Cassie drew in her breath sharply.

"We do not know who our mother is," said Keiron.

She considered this, nodding slightly. "No, and you are not meant to, not yet. I cannot see who she is myself. Her magic is stronger than mine."

There was a long silence after this. The twins did not dare stir under that hypnotic gaze. They became aware that the medicine woman's face was changing. A look of fear, almost terror, stole into it, softening into a deep frown.

"You are at a turning point," she said, "that will lead you into darkness. But you inherited gifts from your hidden mother, and they will help you."

"I wish I could heal my father," Cassie said feelingly.

"You heal the flesh, child, not the mind: that is why you have come."

Cassie flashed her a look. "You know about my gift, then?"

"I know you both have a gift." She shifted and sighed. "You must learn to use your extraordinary gifts wisely – you especially, Cassie, for yours is the more terrible."

There was another silence. "I will help you find the Golden Helmet," she said at last, in a voice so quiet they barely heard it. "For I sense that you two—"

But at this inconvenient point, and much to the twins' dismay, she was interrupted by a rustle of movement at the cave entrance. Tara saw a sea of wolf faces, eyes glowing in the reflected firelight. They beckoned to her. She slipped out and they yelped urgently until she understood.

She crept back in and sidled up to Magda. The twins watched them talk in some unintelligible language.

Magda said, "The wolf-people have made a request and I think it is a wise one." She paused, glancing at Tara. "Shall we say, rather, a bargain."

"What is it?" Cassie asked, flashing Tara an enquiring look.

"Something for something," answered Magda. "You tell them, Tara."

A little nervously, Tara said, "I have told them about the dead wolf-skins we saw in the Ice Castle. They are much excited by them. They want them back."

"But what good are they to them?" asked Keiron.

"They think that, with Cassie's gift, the skins can be brought alive again. They would clothe the wolf-people in the Mansion. The wolf-people would be united once more. You know it's what we've always longed for."

The twins nodded, slightly puzzled.

"They are afraid of the Ice Castle," Tara continued. "It has always been a place of evil for wolf-people. They want you two to fetch the skins from the Ice Castle."

"Your reward," said Magda, putting her arm around Tara, "is my help in finding the Golden Helmet. I think it is a fair deal."

The twins were taken by surprise. They glanced at each other: this was an unwelcome complication.

"But our father's very ill..." Keiron began.

"He needs the potion now," said Cassie at the same time.

"It will take me days to make the potion he needs. Curing the mind is not easy. You have time."

"What if Prince Badrur won't let us have the skins?" Keiron asked.

"Why shouldn't he? They are no good to him."

Keiron turned to his sister. "I think we should do it," he said. "It's what the wolf-people want and we owe it to them, you can see that, can't you? And then Magda will help us find the Golden Helmet."

"Please," said Tara. "It is something my people want more than anything. They are too frightened to go inside the castle itself, it's always been such a place of terror; and now it is too well guarded."

Cassie thought of her father weak and pale on his bed, his mind constantly wandering, and her heart was heavy at such a delay. Her three companions stared at her, each with their own special pleading in their eyes.

"All right," she said, reluctantly. She felt she had no choice.

Before the twins left, Magda gave each of them a fur coat lined with crushed herbs and seeds. "You will need this in that icy castle," she said. Gratefully, the twins put them on.

Then, seeing Will nestling in Keiron's thick flaxen hair, she took hold of him and held him out in the palm of her hand. "Now here's a wise child," she murmured. "You were inspired when you made him. There's more magic in him than in all my potions. Listen to his chatter, won't you." Reluctantly, she handed him back and Will burrowed into the boy's hair, every knot and fibre of his being trembling with delight.

The twins and Tara mounted their horses.

"We will talk of the Helmet when you return with the skins," she called to them.

She was about to return to her cave, but then an extraordinary change came over her. Her body went rigid, struck by a sudden and terrifying vision. She held up her hand for them to halt. She fixed her piercing gaze on Cassie. "Be careful, child," she said in a voice full of foreboding. "Suddenly I see a dark cloud about you, some rash act of generosity that might be your undoing." She pointed a trembling finger accusingly at the girl.

Cassie was so frightened by this sudden change in the medicine woman, she waited no longer. She dug her heels into the horse's flanks and galloped off.

The old woman's words had scared her, but she tried to shrug them off. Why had they trusted her? she asked herself bitterly, her head down, the wind howling in her ears. She has not given us the potion and she has sent us into the camp of the enemy. How then can she point her finger at me?

Keiron drew up beside her.

"We were wrong to go there," she shouted at him. But she knew it was already too late: the wolves were leading them to the Ice Castle, with all its attendant dangers, and the creatures were not to be kept from their prize. She glanced back at Tara and thought the wolf-girl looked taller, more confident than she'd ever seen her before. Even Keiron seemed eager for the challenge. Was it only her that felt like this?

"She will tell us where the Helmet is hidden," Keiron shouted back encouragingly. "All we've got to do is get the wolf-skins. Cheer up, Sis!"

But her thoughts and fears raged as they galloped through wild country the rest of that day. The Ice Castle was several days' journey away over country that none of them knew, and on the third day, aching from so much riding and increasingly hungry, they had to admit they were lost. This was unfamiliar country to this pack of wolves and they were no help.

Towards the end of the fourth day the heavens opened and a rain like icy spears fell relentlessly, drenching them. They were forced to seek shelter under a great tree. The wolf-people huddled together, forlorn and bedraggled. Then some broke away and disappeared among the dripping, hissing trees.

"They are going to look for a village nearby," Tara said, shivering in her drenched furs. "They can smell one not too far off."

A long, uncomfortable hour followed during which the rain turned to sleet and penetrated through layers of fur to the children's shivering skins.

Then through the incessant roar of the sleet and wind they heard faintly the howl of the wolves. The village had been found. Thankfully, the twins followed the wolves' lead. They picked their way through a quagmire of mud and a hissing wood into a clearing. Here village people stood in the doorways of their squat huts. Some came out to make them welcome.

Soon, their identity was known. The children of the Mansion, here in this harsh, forgotten place! Such an honour. The village elder welcomed them into his own spacious cabin and provided them with dry clothes and warm food. Snug at last before a good fire, the twins began to thaw.

"I don't know what we should have done without you," Cassie said to the elder, who smiled at her from a face aged by wind and cruel weather.

"Only the brave or the foolish travel to the Ice Castle," he answered. "And in such weather." He eyed them curiously, pityingly, but he saw they were tired and decided not to tax them with feasts and questions and speeches that night.

Wriggling down into his bed, Keiron said to his sister, to cheer her up, "Tell me what this island will be like when you put the Golden Helmet on your head, and make your wish."

Dreamily, Cassie painted a picture of warmth and light, of vivid colours, of flowers bending in gentle breezes, of fruit hanging ripe, of animals happily rustling in the leaves ... until her brother drifted off into a paradisal dream.

She took longer to get to sleep. Every time she closed her eyes, Magda's accusing finger was pointing at her. Then, when she slipped into darkness, Badrur rode into a grove of her transformed island, dressed all in white and bright with frost, blizzards billowing in his wake.

But dreams were the least of her troubles. On the morrow, in a fit of profound pity, she would do something so terrible even Magda would quake before the dark, blind power that she was about to unleash.

CHAPTER 8

Tara settled down to sleep alongside the twins that night, weary and cold, but sleep would not come. In the light from an oil-lamp she looked on their faces and sadness passed like a wave through her: she would never be fully human. Their looks, their language, their freedom, even their arrogance – she realized then that she was only borrowing these for a while. She rose quietly and lifted the curtain that separated their room from the larger one they had sat in earlier. Only the Elder sat there, smoking a pipe. He smiled at her and beckoned her to sit beside him.

"Well, wolf-child, is it true that you are going to the Ice Castle?"

She nodded.

"And why would anyone want to go to that monstrous place? Do you know, we frighten our children with it? It is not a place I would willingly go to."

She told them about the wolf-skins.

He nodded, understanding. "And where is your skin? Don't you wish you had it now?"

A great longing for it suddenly overcame Tara. It was

not just that it kept out the rain and much of the cold, it was the feeling that without it she was always vulnerable, that she needed its protection.

"I must go," she murmured.

At the door she paused. "Do you have trouble sleeping too?" she asked.

He shook his head. Motioning to another room, he said, "My daughter is about to give birth. The women are all in there. I say it will come tonight, but they do not believe me. We shall see."

Tara ran swiftly across the dark clearing, dodging moonlit puddles, and reached the large log hut where Magda's wolf-people were sleeping. She slipped inside. Although they were not from her pack, the damp smell of her kind welcomed her, and the heaving mass of fur warmed her. Some sleepy wolves made a space for her and she snuggled down with them. For a while she was happy.

But she was aware that she was the only human shape in that hut. She wanted to rouse a few of the younger wolves nearby and ask them to change into their human selves to keep her company, but she was too shy to ask. Must it always be like this, she wondered, neither one thing nor the other?

She eventually drifted into an exhausted and restless sleep.

A piercing scream sliced through the incessant, wavering roar of the wind. Tara sat up. Wolf-people around her sprung to their feet, instantly alert. Was there an attack? Another scream of agony. "It is the woman with child," one of the wolf-women said. They listened in silence as the screams became more rhythmic. "There is something wrong," someone said after a while. "Those are not the ordinary screams of human birth."

Tara thought of the twins. She ran back across the windswept clearing to the Elder's hut. It was full of waiting, whispering, anxious relatives of the Elder and his daughter. She caught sight of the twins, looking pale and fearful, on the far side of the crowd and she worked her way round to join them.

"Where have you been?" Cassie demanded, more from worry than impatience. She took the wolf-girl's hand and squeezed it. She had never been at the birth of a child before and this one seemed fraught with danger.

"Shouldn't we leave them to it?" Keiron whispered. "They won't want to be bothered with us at a time like this." But he made no effort to move.

The screams came more frequently now and the room grew silent. Everyone knew that something terrible was wrong. Their only thought now was what? A dead baby? A deformed one? A twisted womb, putting the mother in mortal danger?

One final scream rent the tense air. Then there was a flurry of voices from the birth room and a sigh of relief went up from the waiting relatives. It is over, came a whispered word, the child is born.

They waited to hear the cry.

Nothing.

In the silence there were sounds of slapping.

Still no cry.

Suddenly the Elder himself arose and burst into

the birth room. He saw a large baby in his wife's arms. It was blue and lifeless.

"She's dead," the Elder's wife wailed.

The mother of the baby looked on, stricken and helpless.

Death of a newborn was an event which, in this village, brought great shame on the family. Death of an Elder's child was a catastrophe. The Elder seized the baby and rocked it back and forth frantically. The child remained lifeless.

The Elder needed more room for what he was going to do next. He barged his way back into the main room. The relatives shuffled back, creating a space.

"What's he going to do?" Keiron whispered.

Cassie didn't answer. In her mind's eye, she had seen what had just happened in the birth room, and *she knew* what was going to happen next. She had a powerful feeling that all this had happened to her before, and she could not understand it. She was tingling all over with a strange kind of energy. She felt on the brink of some dark cliff, and she reached out for Keiron's hand, but he was watching too raptly to notice.

The Elder peeled off the rug in which the baby had been wrapped and threw it aside. He grasped hold of the child's ankles and in a sudden swift movement he began to gyrate, spinning the child around. It was a desperate attempt to force air into the child's lungs, and if it had been an ordinary child it might have worked. Everyone kept their eyes on the spinning baby, praying for signs of life. But then, dizzy and in despair, the Elder slowed to a halt.

The child's silence crushed all hope. The Elder's wife stepped forward and took the baby from him. He let it go with something like disgust, closing his eyes in pain.

"Bury her," he said harshly. "Somewhere deep where no one will discover her."

That word "bury" boomed inside Cassie's head over and over again like a tolling bell until she could bear it no longer. "No," she suddenly screamed. "Let her live."

The crowd of relatives turned and looked at her, horrified. They had forgotten the Mansion's children were there, and they were shamed to think this still-birth had been witnessed by them. The girl was hysterical.

"Be quiet," Keiron hissed, trying to grab hold of his sister.

But she was already hastening forward, pushing her way through the crowd. They would ordinarily have barred her way, but they held back in awe at the extraordinary expression on her face. It blazed with anger, resolve, and above all with pity, and all those who were near her felt singed by it. There was a kind of electric energy around her which made them step back as far as they could as she passed.

Cassie made for the Elder's wife. "Give me the child," she demanded.

She looked at Cassie in amazement.

"*Give me the child*," the girl demanded, her eyes blazing. She held out her hands.

The Elder, sensing something uncanny here, nodded at his wife, and she held out the blue, heavy, waxen-looking baby.

Cassie clasped the child tightly and looked into its closed face. She summoned that mysterious power inside her, which she had known and been shy of since she was tiny, of bringing that which was dead alive once again. Surely this was the greatest use of her power, to bring a dead child back into life? She concentrated so hard she began to shake. She called up the power and chanelled it through her hands into the inert body of the heavy baby.

Keiron and Tara watched her helplessly. Both knew in their bones that she was wrong to do this. Keiron had always understood that Cassie's gift of life stopped at small mammals, that her gift was more for bringing such things as wood and fur alive. Or healing wounds and fractures. But not this. Will too, looked on with horror. No human should meddle so deeply with nature, he muttered to himself over and over as if it was a mantra.

Cassie was now very white and shaking all over. Her eyes were tightly closed in painful concentration. She was pouring her vital life-energy and healing powers into the child.

Everyone who was watching thought they saw the baby begin to move, but it was hard to tell.

Then a scream broke from Cassie and she went still. She opened her eyes and stared down at the baby in her arms. Its eyelids began to flicker. There was a gasp of disbelief. They heard the infant suddenly inhale, a deep rasping sound, and then gasp for more air. A little bubbling murmur came from her lips.

The child's eyes opened. Cassie wiped the traces of mucus that clung to them. The eyes were a dark blackberry colour. Cassie bent over the child and saw an image of herself in those dark eyes, far away, as if she was looking at herself in another dimension. She suddenly felt herself spinning, as if in space, the faces of the pressing crowd around her like wheeling stars, their cries of joy at the child's revival like howling space winds snatching at her hair and limbs. The child's dark eyes were swallowing her up.

Cassie felt drained of all energy, and she took to her bed. Tara never left her side. There was talk of sending for Magda but Cassie, despite the fog in her mind and the extreme fatigue throughout her body, begged them not to. She could not bear the thought of the wise old woman looking down on her in judgement.

For she knew she had done something fundamentally wrong. It was only a feeling then, one of foreboding and dread; it would be some while before she understood the reason.

She was in a strange position. Everyone but Keiron and Tara praised her, blessed her even, for bringing the Elder's granddaughter back from the dead. The child's mother was brought to her bedside and overwhelmed her with tearful gratitude. The Elder pronounced her an Honorary Daughter of the Village which gave her the same status as his own daughters. And there were celebrations which Keiron described to her in detail.

"It is all wrong," she whispered again and again to him in acute embarrassment and remorse.

Keiron, suppressing his doubts, tried to reassure her, to get her to see it from the villagers' point of view. "So you exhausted yourself doing it," he added. "What's a few days in bed?"

"It's not that," she murmured.

"You should be proud of yourself. Bringing a dead baby back to life – wow! That's the sort of thing everyone dreams of being able to do. Think how proud Father will be of you when he hears about it."

That only made her feel worse.

Only Tara really seemed to understand: whenever either of them spoke about the baby they felt each other shudder, like a tremor passing between them. The wolf-girl came to mean more to her in those long agonizing hours than anyone, even her brother.

Keiron became fascinated by the big fat baby. She didn't respond to his cooing and his waggling fingers, but she watched him with large dark eyes. No smile passed her lips, and she hardly moved. She only became animated when food was offered. She devoured everything given to her and seemed to want more and more. And she grew at an extraordinary rate: every day she was noticeably bigger.

Will observed her too. Despite his protests, Keiron lowered the little manikin on to the baby's chest. Will looked into her eyes and saw something of what Cassie had seen too: a vast, cold, empty space where nothing lived, where stars blazed and were consumed in distant galaxies, where the only sound was the howling of cosmic dust storms. He felt he could so easily be sucked into those eyes and be whirled away like tiny flotsam into nothingness. As he sat there, mesmerized by this, the baby reached out and grasped him in a surprisingly quick movement. He felt the life-sap drain out of him. The grasp was crushing. Instinctively, he knew that if he struggled she would crush the life out of him completely.

Help! he managed to shout to Keiron.

With difficulty the boy prised Will from the baby's hand. She turned to stare at him, a look of fury in her dark eyes, and Keiron stepped back, amazed.

Cassie should never have brought that little monster back from the dead, Will gasped. Keiron slid him into his pocket where he curled silent and scared for the next twenty-four hours.

Cassie, nourished by herbal broths and the most succulent cuts of deer steak, was soon able to get up and resume her life. Her body recovered quickly, but the dark shadow of her deed stretched over her soul all day and even into her sleep. She thought of Magda's accusing finger and she writhed in the echo of her warning. Why did she feel like this? she wondered. Hadn't she done what everyone would have done, given her powers?

She avoided seeing the baby.

Tara told her of a strange incident: a bird had perched on the baby's cot. With amazing swiftness, the baby had seized it, gurgled delightedly as it struggled, then, when it pecked her, she squeezed the life out of it. As it died, Tara reported, wide-eyed with horror, *the baby seemed to grow visibly bigger*.

The child is feeding on death, Cassie said to herself, and the thought twisted like a knife inside her. Now she began to understand the enormity of her mistake.

So she struggled in her mind. When the time came for them to leave, she began to think that, if she saw the baby alive, she might be able to convince herself that what she had done was right. To forgive herself.

"Should I?" she asked Tara.

The wolf-girl shook her head. But Keiron urged her to.

The wolf-people were assembled, ready to leave. Keiron was about to leap on to his horse. The Elder and his family had already said their farewells. Yet she hesitated. The child's mother saw her hesitate and knew what held her back. She slipped away and came back with the baby in her arms.

"How heavy she is already," she said fondly, looking into the child's impassive face. "She is growing so fast." She held out the child to Cassie. "Here, say farewell to her. She's almost as much your child as mine now."

Cassie approached the child, her heart beating erratically, the blood draining from her face.

The girl with the gift of life met the cold, dark stare of the child brought back from the dead. It was like a silent test of wills, lasting only a few seconds but seeming to stretch for ever. Cassie shuddered; she knew for certain then that she had released some dark, blind force into the world and that she would in time be punished for it.

She wrenched herself away from the child's implacable gaze and looked aghast at her brother. Then she cried, great sobbing gasps that amazed the on-lookers. "I'm sorry, I'm sorry," she kept repeating, to everyone's distress, until the chant was silenced by Tara who pressed the girl tightly to her and calmed her down.

As soon as they had cleared the village, a wispy fog descended. Trees and rocks, shaking in the gusts of wind, looked like agitated ghosts. The wolf-people kept their noses to the ground and guided Tara and the twins through the fog. It was a subdued party and no one spoke. Cassie's sobs had had a cleansing effect on the girl and now she felt scoured and empty.

But her ordeal that morning was not yet over.

Suddenly, the wolf-people lifted their heads, sensing someone ahead. They swarmed around a looming spectre in their path. The twins and Tara pulled up and slid from their mounts.

Magda, the medicine woman, stood in their path. Word had got back to her of the child's resurrection. She had been so angry, so disturbed at this misuse of Cassie's power, she felt she had to set out to confront the girl. Cassie felt the full force of her disapproval.

"I'm sorry," she whispered. "I didn't know."

"I warned you," said Magda. "And now it is my duty to spell out to you just what you have done."

Keiron, distressed at the look of shock on his sister's face, stepped between her and Magda. "Look," he protested, "she only did what anyone would have done in her situation. She saved the child's life. Why is that so terrible?"

"She scorned the laws of Nature," Magda replied sternly. "She went against its divine will."

"So?" said Keiron, fearful of this woman but made bold by his sister's helplessness. "Isn't that what *you* do all the time, with your potions and spells?"

She glared dismissively at him. "I work *with* Nature, not against it."

Goaded by this, Cassie pushed her brother aside and said in desperation, "Isn't that what I did too?"

Magisterially, Magda shook her great mane of hair. "Nature wanted that child dead."

"Why?" Keiron almost shouted.

"It is not for us to question Her," Magda answered vehemently.

"I do not understand," Cassie wailed.

Magda allowed some pity into her gaze. "Then let me explain," she said, impatient at having to spell out what to her was obvious. "That child's soul had already fled by the time she was born. It does not matter why. When you brought her back to life, *she was born without a soul*."

Those words seemed to hang in the foggy air, over the motionless bodies of the wolf-people who were listening to every word of this intently, over the heads of the silent horses, among the dripping trees. Even the wind had died to a soft moan. *She was born without a soul.*

"What does that mean?" Cassie whispered.

"Don't tell her," Keiron pleaded.

But the old woman ignored him. "It means that she will grow monstrous. She will devour life. She will feed on death. Do not be fooled by her appearance. She will be invincible, for nothing short of the great power of the gods will be able to withstand her."

Cassie held herself tightly. "I did not know," she whispered.

"I came here to accuse you," said Magda, her voice softening with pity. "But I see I had no need to. You accuse yourself. Poor child."

Unexpectedly, the tall, old woman drew Cassie to her and stroked her head, comfortingly. "You were caught in a trap," she murmured.

"Poor Cass," said Keiron, standing helpless by her side.

"Well, I have had my say," Magda said with a sigh. "You don't know what evil you have set in train... But so be it, you were used. Now, go, fetch those wolf-skins."

"And our father?" Keiron asked.

"Don't worry. He's in no immediate danger."

The twins mounted their horses and the wolf-people began to swarm forward.

The medicine woman turned to Keiron. "I will help you find the Helmet," she said, knowing that this was his greatest preoccupation. "In time, Cassie might redeem herself through it. Go quickly now, and avoid that prince, for he will dog your footsteps wherever you go."

CHAPTER 9

The following days of travel through a land that grew colder and colder were miserable even for the wolf-people who were used to the terrain and the climate. For a few hours a white, diffused sun struggled against heavy grey clouds and patches of freezing fog, but mostly the wind hurled rain, sleet, dead leaves and twigs at them and contested every step they made. It was difficult to find enough food for the horses – the supplies they had brought had to be eked out – and the animals were becoming exhausted. For two days they sheltered in a damp cave where cold, lizard-like creatures sat on ledges and in crevices staring at them with glassy eyes.

Cassie remained grimly silent. She brushed aside attempts at sympathy from Keiron or Tara. The moment she had brought that monstrous child alive, she had stepped through an invisible barrier, leaving her childhood behind: she sensed this all the time. It was why she was so brusque with her brother – his innocence shone like a rebuke in her eyes and made her feel sick with longing.

The wolf-people sat patiently at the entrance to the cave. They did not like this delay but knew the frailty of humans. Nor did they like the country they were in, or their destination, but there was an expectant fever in their veins which kept them going, for were they not at last on the trail of the missing wolf-skins? For more than a century those missing skins had stained the honour of the wolf-people, forcing them to accept servitude in the Mansion and the nakedness of humans. Even Magda's divining powers had been no match for the impenetrable walls of the Ice Castle, protected by who knows what evil magic. The wolf-people were impatient to be off, to find the skins, but Tara pleaded with them to have patience. Remember, she said, only Cassie can bring the skins alive: they needed her.

Some of them watched Tara closely. They could see that she was on the human side of the line that divided the two species. It happened sometimes, wolves born to be human, but they always suffered for it in the end; they pitied her. But some envied her too, for in her human form she seemed freer than they were, more easy in her body. Indeed, a stranger would not have guessed that she was a wolf-girl except by the slant of her amber eyes and by certain wolfish gestures, the way she twitched her head or raised her nose to sniff the air.

Keiron and Will were perhaps the most contented. Keiron found a quiet and steely enjoyment in their new-found independence, away from the strict eye of their father, the surly disapproval of Aulic, the routine of the Mansion. The exciting events of the past few days, however frightening for his sister, filled his veins with a kind of fever for more. This was life! And the prospect of finding the Golden Helmet! Did Magda really know where it might be?

"When we find the Helmet," he said to Cassie, trying to find a way to pierce her gloom, "we shall live in perpetual sunlight. Just think of it!"

Cassie knew he was trying to cheer her up, and for that reason she was inclined to ignore him; but even in the darkness of her self-recrimination, his words warmed her, and she gave him a weak smile.

As they travelled to the northernmost tip of the island, Magda's accusing finger seemed to hover before her all the time. Her mental pain was reflected in bodily exhaustion. She did not complain but Keiron and Tara began to get worried. They thought her best prospects lay in getting to the castle as soon as possible, to throw themselves on the mercy of Angharer, the prince's aunt, despite the risk that Badrur might be there. So they pressed on through steady drizzles of freezing rain until at last the castle loomed against the metal-grey sky.

Rough-looking men stood either side of the gates and let them file past, watching them suspiciously: to them all visitors were potential enemies. As soon as the last wolf was in the courtyard, they closed the great doors. Angharer, appearing on the balcony, shouted to one of the men to bring the children up to her at once.

The twins climbed the steps to the great hall. Tara tried to follow them but her way was barred.

"She must come with us," Cassie demanded.

"Not my orders," said the man who was barring her way. "The wolf-people are to be housed in the stables where we can keep an eye on them."

"But she is our friend," Keiron protested.

The man made a contemptuous noise. "She said bring up the children. Those are my orders. You heard them," he said, and he pushed Tara back into the pack of silent wolf-people.

"Don't worry, Tara," Cassie shouted. "You'll be safer with the wolf-people."

They climbed the remaining steps to the hall.

Cassie took off her sodden fur hood. "My child," said Angharer, "you look quite ill. The journey must have been too much. I can't think why you have come so far out of your way. Surely not just to visit me?"

"I do feel faint," Cassie whispered. To see a fire blazing in a fireplace, to be inside solid walls among human furnishings, to hear a sympathetic voice – it was too much for her. She slumped on to a chair and let her head fall on the table. "I'm sorry," she murmured, "but I'm so tired."

"She was taken ill a few days ago," Keiron explained. "We thought the best thing was to throw ourselves on your mercy."

Angharer showed Cassie to a small room where there was a bed. Hastily they made it up and Cassie gratefully got into it. She knew she was acting pathetically, but for once she didn't care; all she wanted was sleep and forgetfulness.

Back in the hall, Keiron sat at the table. He felt a bit awkward to be alone with this forbidding, lonely woman. But Angharer, starved of visitors, set herself to make the most of this unexpected guest, even if he was only a boy. Perhaps a visit to the Mansion might come out of it.

"You look hungry," she said. "Let me get you something to eat."

A servant brought in platters of cold meat, a soft watery cheese, some hard bread and a flagon of crab-apple juice, which Keiron soon set to with gusto. He had got tired of the dried meat they had been eating in the last few days and the strange tastes of the brooks they had drunk from. As his stomach warmed with food, so he warmed to the woman who watched over him.

Don't tell her anything about the baby, Will warned.

But I've got to tell her something.

Tell her why you've come. The wolf-skins are no good to her.

"I'm surprised your father let you out on your own," Angharer said. "What was he thinking of?"

"He is not well. We went out to find Magda the medicine woman and ask her for some potions."

"And did you find her?"

"We did."

"Then why aren't you back with your father?"

"She insisted on us coming here first."

"Oh?" said Angharer, her face growing suspicious. "Why was that?"

"She wants the wolf-skins. You know, the ones we saw hanging in that room?"

"Oh, does she? Whatever for?"

"She's friends with the wolf-people. They want them back. Can we have them? They're no good to you, are they? The wolf-people would be your friends for life if you let them have them."

Angharer sensed some lever here which might

advance her own position. "We shall see," she said. "Naturally, I shall have to speak to my nephew about them. Strictly speaking, they are his skins, not mine."

Keiron nodded glumly. He seized a leg from some unidentifiable carcass and took a mouthful of succulent meat. Things were more complicated than he had imagined. He knew then that if Badrur refused to let them have the skins, he and Cassie would somehow have to get the wolf-people into the castle secretly to steal them; there were too many for them to smuggle out unseen. And with so many suspicious men about, that would be dangerous.

Soon after, he managed to slip away. At last, he was free to search the castle: the Golden Helmet might just be here. The next few hours were eerie and fascinating: it was like wandering through a lumber room of nightmares and centuries of forgotten life. He searched doggedly everywhere until darkness defeated him.

The following morning he visited Cassie first thing. He told her about his futile search for the Helmet and about his fears that they might have to try and smuggle out the wolf-skins. They spoke in murmurs, fearful of being overheard. Then Cassie got out of bed and stood unsteadily. "I feel much better this morning," she said, although she did not look it. "I'm going to bring those pelts alive. Every one of them, if I can." There was a sudden determination in her pale face.

"I'll come and help you."

"No, you go and be with Tara. She'll be frightened. Tell her we'll try and get the skins out somehow. The wolf-people must be getting frantic wondering what's going on."

Keiron found Tara in the gloom of a tall stone barn, surrounded by wolf-people. She was the only one in human form, it being too cold for the others to shed their skins. He explained the situation. His news was not to the wolf-people's liking and there was much angry yapping.

Keiron and Tara decided to examine the stone monsters more closely. They had seen many of the smaller petrified creatures within the castle walls; what Keiron wanted to look at was the monstrous ones in the trees outside. They found a rotting door that easily splintered; it led down a dripping passage to the disused moat outside. Here they saw huge, amphibious creatures staring sightless in the mud, their webbed feet and mossed skins hinting at the green depths of the long-dried-up waters that once surrounded the castle. Climbing the steep side of the moat, they found themselves in a sparse copse of gaunt, stunted trees dusted with snow. Great rocky mounds loomed everywhere. Brushing the snow from some of these, they stared into glassy eyes, at bent talons, at broken leathery wings, at the pattern of scales, at crushed fins and crests, at huge bellies and heavy feet. Jaws, still intact and filled with dirt and dead leaves, yawned cavernously, their teeth like icicles, the beasts frozen in the act of bellowing in agony.

And then, turning a corner of the castle, Keiron came across the biggest monster of them all, a giant salamander, pictures of which his father had shown him many times. It reared on its hind legs like some great dragon, its body twisting in defiance, its talons clawing the air. Keiron remembered the sketch he had drawn, the planets he had joined up with a pencil line, on that day in his father's study when Lord Tancred had read the stars and predicted catastrophes. Well, this monster was in league with the stars, Keiron thought: there's something unearthly about it.

Tara, who had strayed behind Keiron, was caught unawares by the great looming creature. She looked up at it before she could stop herself, then cried out and turned away, shuddering.

"Don't be afraid," said Keiron. "It can't hurt you."

"It can," she said. "There is a wolf-legend that says, when the great salamander comes alive, thousands of wolf-people will die. It curses all those who look at it." She trembled violently. Keiron led her away from the monster, back towards the door through which they came.

In the afternoon, as Keiron and Tara were studying a petrified insect with a fat body and a row of stings sticking jagged and broken from its legs, there came the sound of shouting from the battlements. "The prince is coming. Open the gates."

Keiron and Tara ran to a buttress where they could hide from view and watch the track to the castle gates. Presently there came the soft thud of horse's hooves and Prince Badrur hove into view, his black cloak billowing out like bats' wings. In his wake were a few of his men.

"Maybe we'll get our answer about the wolf-skins sooner than we thought," said Keiron. "You go and tell the wolf-people. I'll tell Cassie. With any luck, we'll leave this horrible place today."

He swallowed hard. He was about to confront the man who had tried to poison his father's mind. And he had to hide what he felt. But if they could get the wolf-skins from him for Magda and her wolves, he would be one step nearer finding the Golden Helmet. For Cassie's sake, that was now so important: and who knew what wonderful powers she might release though it. He took a deep breath and stepped boldly out from behind the buttress.

CHAPTER 10

While Keiron and Tara were out exploring, Cassie was in the large round chamber where the wolf-skins hung. Hooked on to rafters, they were just too high for her to reach. She looked for the one she had brought alive but it was no longer there.

She went to the window and peered out. Down below, among the snow-laden trees, she caught a glimpse of her brother and the wolf-girl. Keiron was swinging on a branch, bringing cascades of snow down on Tara, who was shrieking in protest, and for the first time since *the baby*, as she referred to the event, she smiled.

She looked at the dead skins hanging like shadows without bodies and thought, I must bring them alive too. But now she was so nervous of her power it took her a long time to summon the courage to do it. She found a pile of mouldering books in what she supposed was once the library and staggered with them up to the chamber. Standing on the books, she was able to stroke the skins. She felt the electric energy stir and flow within her, pass though her fingers and into the pelts. The stiffness of the skin melted into softness, the hairs turned from bristles to sable, the whole became supple and fresh. She stroked and dreamed and as each pelt was brought back to life, shining softly in the dim light, she felt her own bruised spirit begin to revive, as if she was stroking life back into herself.

Keiron was called into the great hall. Prince Badrur stood by the fire, his face white and impassive, drops of water in the mane of his thick black hair. Badrur welcomed him with a cold smile and said, "I am glad that you sought refuge in my castle. My aunt has told me something of your trials, and how you have made yourself at home here." His eyes glinted darkly in the firelight.

"Thank you," said Keiron, trying to hide his distrust.

"He is a good child," said Angharer. "He prefers the outdoor life – like you did, Badrur, at the same age; he likes to test his courage wherever he is. Is that not so, Keiron?"

He nodded warily. "I like riding and hunting and exploring. I don't mind sleeping in huts and caves."

"What about the animals?" Badrur asked, his eyes softly gleaming. "Do they do as you tell them?"

Keiron faltered. "I don't understand."

"When I was your age, I could make animals jump and spin and try to fly just by staring into their eyes. Hypnotism, you see. It gave me endless amusement. You don't have this gift?"

Keiron couldn't help recoiling.

Badrur's eyes resumed their coldness. "Well, my aunt has told me why you are here," he said briskly.

"I am sorry to hear of your father's illness. I cannot say that I'm surprised about it, he was pushing himself too hard."

Keiron turned to Angharer. "Have you told him about the wolf-skins?"

"Ah, the wolf-skins," he interrupted. "I presume the medicine woman wants them in exchange for your father's potions?"

"Yes," Keiron nodded, keeping a straight face.

"The wolf-skins are no good to us. But perhaps they were put there for a purpose? Until I find out what that might be..." he shrugged.

Keiron knew better than to plead.

"And where is Cassandra?" Badrur suddenly demanded, as if affronted by her absence.

"I've told you," Angharer protested. "She's not well. The journey..."

"That's right," said Keiron. "I expect she's in her room."

"Then we shall give her a pleasant surprise."

Keiron followed the prince along the winding passages, apprehensive for his sister. Why was he so interested in Cassie?

Her room was empty. He seemed annoyed. "Where is she?" he wondered aloud. Keiron shrugged. "I can guess," Badrur muttered, and he swept out.

They climbed the winding steps to the round chamber. There they discovered Cassie standing on a pile of books clasping a soft pelt. She looked as if she had been caught in some misdeed.

"Cassandra! So it is true," said the prince, striding in and stroking one of the pelts that had been transformed by her touch. "You have the gift of life."

Cassie stepped down from the books, glancing fearfully at her brother.

"He guessed you were here," Keiron whispered. "I didn't have time..."

"No need for that," said Badrur. "She is doing no wrong. Come here, Cassie. I want to look into your eyes."

Reluctantly, Cassie obeyed. He lifted her head. She looked into dark eyes that seemed to grow and fill with stars. She felt a sense of being sucked in and she resisted. Her spirit curled itself tightly like a deep root that would not budge.

He pushed her aside and a dark look of frustration came into his face. "You have a stronger will than your brother," he observed.

He went to the window and brooded there for a while.

The twins huddled together. They were only too well aware of his dangerous unpredictability.

Keiron felt Will trembling in his breast pocket. *Don't resist him too much,* was all the advice that the manikin could muster.

Abruptly, Badrur turned to face them, his face now flickering with wild and destructive thought. "Since I left your father's house," he said, "I have been searching for clues to the whereabouts of the Golden Helmet. And do you know what my instinct tells me?"

They shook their heads fearfully.

"That it'll take magic to find it. And who has magic on this island? Your father – but I have seen the extent of his, it is not much. Magda, the medicine woman – who knows more than anyone..." A flash of annoyance made him turn and pace the room; he punched his fist against his hand several times. "And you two." He fixed his gaze on Keiron. "Though precisely what your magic is I'm not quite sure," he added.

He stared at them, his eyes gathering light. His face took on a cruel, intent aspect; the twins drew together. "I could kill you both now," he said quietly. "Hang you from these rafters like these skins and watch you swing."

The twins gasped. They pressed against the wall, their hearts thudding hard.

"With you dead, and your father soon to be, the Mansion would be mine. Soon, the island would be mine too."

"No one would follow you," Cassie hissed at him.

"They would have no choice. One glance into the eye of any creature on this island, and their will evaporates like that." He made a dismissive gesture with his hand. "Ever after, they are my slaves. You have not seen this power yet."

"Why should we believe you?" Keiron said hotly.

Badrur laughed. "It's nothing to me whether you do or not. But let me amuse you with this. Behind these walls there lurk rats and mice and other vermin. Watch."

His face seemed to set into stone and his eyes began to blaze with a cold blue radiating energy. The twins instinctively closed their eyes. They felt their spirits being sucked towards some chasm, and they had to resist with all their might. *Hang on*, Will said, feeling like one clinging to a cliff edge.

Presently, they became aware of high-pitched

screeching and squealing, of the scuffling of many tiny paws on the wooden floor. On opening their eyes they saw a swarm of little creatures, rats, mice, large beetles, lizards, toads, crowding around the prince and looking up at him with slavish eyes.

Prince Badrur extinguished the radiating light in his eyes and laughed. "You see. Just a minor demonstration. Now, if all these creatures were great lumbering bears or wolves or snow-leopards, what then, eh?"

The prince smiled to himself again. He strode to the window and with his bare fist he knocked a hole in the thick pane of glass. "Out," he commanded the animals. In an orderly file, they swarmed up the wall, wriggled through the hole and hurled themselves into oblivion.

Now the twins felt truly frightened. They backed into the corner of the room. "Let us out," Keiron demanded ineffectually.

"So you see," said Badrur with satisfaction. "I can control the animal kingdom. With the Golden Helmet, I could control everything else, I'm sure of it."

He toyed with their fear.

Then he changed tack. "I had a strange experience on the way here," he said. "Are you listening to me, Cassandra? I came to a village. In the centre of this village I was amazed to see a giant baby. She was learning to walk on her stumpy legs. The villagers were watching her, and I could see that she frightened them. What little monster is this? I asked, and do you know what they told me?"

Cassie wailed softly, caught by a sudden spasm of pain.

"They said the daughter of the Mansion had brought this child back from the dead. How so, I wondered? How can she reverse nature like this? Do you have this power?"

Cassie moaned again.

"Leave her alone," Keiron muttered, trying to comfort her.

"So I went up to this child. She rose before me like a dog on its hind legs and I looked into her eyes, thinking to give her a little surprise..." He paused here and his face hardened. "But do you know what I saw? Vast dark skies, infinite space; it was like looking into a cold, dead universe. I sucked a bit of that into myself before I could prevent it."

Cassie knew exactly what he was talking about.

"Truly, you brought a monster back to life, Cassandra. Did you know that?"

"I could not help it," she protested. "I thought she was an ordinary child."

"There's nothing ordinary about her. She is growing at a rate a hundred times faster than any other baby. She already has great strength. She slobbered all over me and would not let me go. I tried to hypnotize her but she resisted. And now..."

His voice faltered. In a sudden hoarse whisper, he added, "Now she is attached to me. Something passed between us... Horrible! Vile! *What have you done, Cassandra?*"

Cassie lowered herself to the floor and began to sob.

"Leave her alone," Keiron pleaded again.

"Oh, but she should be pleased," he said. "It's because of this demonstration of her power that I will let her live. Such a power is too rare to be thrown away. Who knows what use I might put it to when I take over this island?" He paused, a smile passing over his lips. "As for you, boy…" he said. He looked pointedly at the rafters. "If you can prove some similar power… Otherwise…" His white face broke into a grin and his hands moved back and forth imitating the movement of a body hanging from the rafters.

Keiron felt the hands of death brush over his soul. *What shall I do, Will?* he cried out in his head.

Make his clothes speak to you, Will said urgently.

Keiron knew that in the next few minutes his life would hang in the balance. His mind raced. He focused on the prince's boots. *Where do you come from?* he asked desperately, and they answered him.

"Those," he said pointing at the boots, "were cut by yourself from an alligator's skin. You wrestled with the creature in a pool, at your mother's summer palace, for the entertainment of her guests, and then you skinned it, dried it, and cut from it a dozen pairs of boots."

Badrur looked from his boots to the boy in amazement.

"And that cloak," Keiron continued, getting into his stride. "It was made from a great kite your grandfather once made. That kite killed him in an electric storm: the current shot down the wire cord and turned him into a heap of charcoal."

Badrur laughed in surprise.

"Oh, and that salamander pendant round your neck," Keiron gabbled on, "you extracted the talon in the locket from…"

"Enough!" Prince Badrur ordered. "I don't know how

you could possibly know these things." He regarded the boy with a grudging respect. "How do you do it?"

"Things speak to me," Keiron said, relief flooding through him. "They have voices which I hear."

"You should have told me earlier about your gift."

"I didn't know I'd have to fight for my life then," Keiron shouted, suddenly enraged.

Hold on, Will urged. Keiron clenched his teeth.

"Well, you have talked yourself out of danger. My aunt was right, you have courage." He went over to them and held out his hands. "Do not cower before me any more," he said. "We three are marked out with special powers. We three are of a kind. I will spare you. Indeed, I will ask you to forgive me for the fright I have given you. It is only my way. Only a game I play. Come, do you forgive me?"

The twins were so confused by such a rapid change in their antagonist, all they could do was nod.

"Now tell me," he said in an insinuating voice. "What was the bargain you made with Magda?"

He saw the look of dismay that passed between them and he knew that he had guessed correctly. "She's not just giving you some medicine, is she?"

The twins tried to look puzzled.

"Don't try and fool me. She knows where the Helmet is, doesn't she? And she's going to tell you in return for the skins."

"We don't know," Cassie protested.

"I don't believe you," he hissed into their faces. "Now listen, here's a little bargain. I'll let you have these wolf-skins, you tell me what Magda knows about the Helmet, eh?"

The twins looked at each other, saw a way out of their predicament, and turned back to him. "Yes," said Keiron, "we will do it. But if Magda has nothing much to tell us..."

"Oh, but she has. She's hiding something, I know it."

He opened the door. "Well, we must delay no longer. We will set off at once for the medicine woman. I would not like to think your father has died for want of her potions. Come, stir yourselves. We shall be leaving later today."

He laughed aloud, then strode out.

The twins felt too scared and weak to do anything for a while but lean against the wall by the window in silence. Keiron kept his arm tightly around his sister.

"We must cut the skins down," she said at last, looking up into the rafters. "Can you climb up there while I bring the last of them alive?"

"If he gets hold of the Helmet," said Keiron, "he'd have all the power he wants. He'd make everyone do his bidding, just like those poor animals that fell to their death down there. This island would be a never-ending nightmare."

"And we would not survive in it."

In silence, they managed to cut down the wolf-skins. As Keiron undid the knots that tied them, he could not help thinking of his own body hanging from these same rafters. *Too close for comfort*, he said to Will.

Late that afternoon, a cart was loaded with the pelts in the courtyard. Cassie, exhausted and fearful, snuggled into them with Tara. Their horses were tethered to the cart and Keiron rode behind it. Prince Badrur took the reins, while a posse of his men rode on ahead. The wolf-people, excited by the sight of the missing wolf-skins, swarmed around the cart.

Prince Badrur cracked the whip. He felt that at last he was on the trail that would lead him to the Golden Helmet: his dark powers would then know no limits.

The days they spent travelling to Magda were strange and tense. The twins felt Badrur watching them all the time, toying with them like a wild cat might play with a wood-mouse before devouring it. He seemed amused by the state of fear he put them in. When they camped at night in villages, the fear spread further among the people. He had only to demonstrate his hypnotic power on their animals and they shivered, as if a shadow was passing over their souls.

Cassie found comfort in bringing each of the wolf-skins alive. She took each one from the great mound on the cart and felt her energy flow into it, felt it come alive in her hands.

On the third night of their journey Badrur overheard Tara say to Keiron, "Well, he'll never be able to control the wolf-people. The human in us is our protection."

That was like a challenge. He summoned to his cabin wolf after wolf. They emerged dazed and exhausted by the tussle of wills that ensued, but they resisted. The wolf-people resented this assault upon their independence. It was a mistake that would cost Badrur dear in the turbulent times ahead.

As they neared Magda's cave, some wolves went on ahead to bring news of their approach. There was great excitement at the return of the missing wolf-skins, and as the party cantered up to the cave entrance it was swarming with yapping wolf-people, many of them in human form.

Magda's face became impassive when she saw Badrur.

"What have you to do with these children?" she demanded.

"They sought my protection," he answered blithely. "You wouldn't deny them that, I hope?"

"Then you won't mind waiting while I take them inside. They don't have quite your resistance to the cold." She ushered the twins into her cave. The wolf-people closed ranks behind them, blocking Badrur's path, but he did not seem to care.

"I thank you for the wolf-skins," Magda said to the twins. "They will end half a century of humiliation for the wolf-people. Oh, I know your family took them in and sheltered them, and they will be eternally on your side for that, but their spirits have long been tarnished by such subservience. Your father will have to get himself a new set of servants."

"I'm sure there will be plenty of village people who will take their place," said Keiron.

Magda scrutinized Cassie. "You have been through dark days, child. Don't brood on them. There is a greater force for life in you than that which you gave to the monstrous baby, believe me. I have had fearful dreams, I see such turbulence to come on this island, but in all of them you are there, radiating what is good, what is *balanced*. My dreams may be puzzling but they never deceive. Now come on, cheer up. You'll need all your strength for the battles ahead."

"Battles? What battles?" Keiron asked.

But she ignored him. "Here," she said, shuffling over to a stone shelf, "is the medicine for your father." She handed over an earthenware bottle. "My wolf-people brought me samples of what was in that hookah he was smoking, and I have made an antidote to it. They tell me that he has relapses and remains feeble, but this potion should set him back on his feet. Give him two thimblefuls a day, that's all he needs."

"I'll give them to him myself," said Cassie, taking the bottle gratefully.

Magda gestured to the cave entrance and lowered her voice. "But why is he with you? He can never be a friend of yours."

"We know," said Keiron with a wry grin.

"We cannot shake him off," said Cassie anxiously. "He watches us all the time. He wants to take over the Mansion and rule the island. He wants the power of the Helmet... But the villagers are bound to be on our side," she added. "So he has no real power, has he?"

"And the wolf-people resist him, they will not be hypnotized by him," said Keiron gleefully.

"He is getting impatient," Cassie said, looking out of the cave entrance. The prince was rearing his horse against the wall of wolf-people, cursing them. "He thinks you will tell us where the Golden Helmet is. That's what he's waiting for."

Magda folded the girl in her arms. "Get those pelts back to the naked wolves in the Mansion," the old woman said. "I only wish I could be there to see their faces!"

"But won't you tell us where the Helmet is?" Keiron pleaded.

She shook her head. "Not with him out there."

Keiron's heart sank, but he knew she was right.

There was a sudden increase in the yelping of the wolves. Badrur had dismounted and was hacking his way through the animals.

"Let him through," Magda cried, and the wolves fell back.

The prince loomed in the cave entrance. "Well," he said to Magda. "Are you ready to tell me where you think the Golden Helmet is hidden?"

She returned his gaze, stony-faced.

He cursed her. He kicked at her pots and cauldrons and tore at the dried plants and haunches that hung from the ceiling. The wolves snarled, ready to pounce on him, but seeing a ring of his men advancing towards the cave with knives and swords, Magda held them back.

Then Badrur, on an angry impulse, seized Cassie and held a knife to her throat. There was a horrible silence. Cassie, her eyes closed, shook all over.

Magda glared at him. "All I know," she hissed, "is that it is buried with the dead, like a death's head itself."

"You can do better than that! Where?"

She shrugged angrily. "In the Mansion. Or in the Ice Castle. Somewhere where men bury their dead."

They continued to glare at each other, like a duel with eyes. Then Badrur threw Cassie aside, calculating that he had gained all he could from the medicine woman.

At last they reached the high ridge that looked down on the Mansion far below, with the surf-crested sea beyond it. The twins felt profoundly relieved to see it.

"You needn't come any further," Cassie said boldly to Badrur. "My father will hardly make you welcome after all that you have done."

He laughed harshly. "Ridiculous child!" He manoeuvred his horse next to Cassie's and to her horror he snatched the bag containing the potion from its hook on the saddle.

"You would not be so ... so mean," Keiron shouted in disbelief.

Badrur tossed the bottle up and down in his hand. "A simple bargain. That's all I'm asking."

The wind howled about them.

"What?" asked Cassie at last.

"You know what I want."

"But we don't know where it is," said Keiron.

"Perhaps not," he answered. "But you have a gift, boy, which can be used to find it – if it is in the Mansion. You must ask every wall, step, banister, everything, until the Helmet's hiding place is revealed."

CHAPTER 11

The news that the twins had returned with the missing skins spread like a rapid wind through the Mansion. The wolf-people swarmed out into the courtyard even as the twins were dismounting from their horses. Tara stayed on the cart on which the pelts were piled and held one up triumphantly. "We found them in the Ice Castle," she shouted, "and Cassie has brought them to life for you." The wolf-people swarmed about the cart, seizing skins, trying them on, putting them aside to find a better fit, and soon there was quite a scrum. Keiron would have liked to have stayed to watch it, but Cassie urged him inside.

As they climbed the stairs to their father's room, Keiron looked out of each window, down into the courtyard, and each time he looked he saw that more and more of the wolf-people were no longer humans but wolves. The pack down there was getting bigger and bigger. Tara alone remained human, not searching for a skin for herself.

Cassie was burning with anxiety about their father. The twins ran down the long gloomy passage to his room. Just as they approached it the door opened.

To their horror, who should emerge from the room but – Aulic!

"Ah, dear children," said Aulic with a welcome-back smile, his squat little goblin-like body writhing with the effort of it. "You have returned at last. I have been keeping an eye on your father while…"

"You should not be here," Cassie said fiercely.

"Not after what you've done," Keiron added, clenching his fists.

He covered his surprise and feigned puzzlement. "I cannot think what you mean. Your arduous journey must have distressed you."

"Let us pass."

"Of course. Your father is most anxious to see you."

"And go from this house at once," Cassie demanded. "We don't want you here."

His face darkened. "That is for your father to decide. Not his… And your father has every confidence in me."

"Not for much longer," said Keiron grimly.

Aulic began to step aside, then he froze. He looked down the passage. They turned and saw Prince Badrur there, glowering at them all.

"Remember our little bargain," the prince called out. "Come to my room when you have seen your father. Aulic, come with me!"

Badrur turned and disappeared down a passage to his room. Aulic pushed past them and scampered after him.

Their father, having heard their voices, was attempting to rise from his bed. The twins rushed to him and he managed to fold both of them in his arms.

They did not know how much they had missed him until that moment. He looked much better than when they had last seen him.

"You have been gone much longer that any of us reckoned."

"We'll tell you about that later, Father. We've got some medicine from Magda. She is sure you're being poisoned by Aulic and she has given us antidotes."

"Poisoned by Aulic? What makes you say that?"

"Through this," said Cassie, pointing at the hookah at the side of his bed. "The stuff you smoke affects your mind and makes you ill. Magda is sure of it."

He sank back on to the bed, looking surprised. "What tales has she been filling your head with?"

"It's true, Father," said Keiron. "Aulic is in league with Prince Badrur. . ."

"Oh, and is he against me too?" Lord Tancred interrupted with a disbelieving chuckle.

The twins looked at each other. They saw they had a lot of ground to cover with their father. "Prince Badrur has the medicine," Cassie said, cutting to the quick. "He snatched it from us. He won't let you have it unless we help him find the Golden Helmet."

"Ah," said Tancred, rubbing his chin. "That's taking his mission a bit too far, perhaps. But I'm sure he'll see sense when I speak to him."

He rose to call the prince. The twins had to stand in his path to restrain him. "Listen to us first," Keiron pleaded. *"He threatened to kill us."*

At last they had his full attention. He listened intently to their story, his brow growing cold, anger kindling in his heart. They left nothing out: the discovery of his unconscious body in the locked chapel, the bargain they struck with Magda to retrieve the missing wolf-skins, the resurrection of the dead child, the wolf-skins in the castle, Badrur's threats, his hypnotic power over the animals, his absolute desire for the Golden Helmet and the power it would bring him to take over the island.

When they had finished, Tancred rose from his bed and in a smouldering silence he put on his great robe. He looked around for something he might brandish as a weapon. For a few seconds he contemplated a sword on the wall, but settled for a cane with a gold lizard-headed top instead.

"Wait here," he commanded.

"But you can't go on your own."

"I am not afraid of him," Lord Tancred said contemptuously. "Stay here."

But the twins could see how weak he was. They ignored this command and stole behind him as he made his way to Prince Badrur's room.

He pushed open the door. Prince Badrur was puffing one of his hookahs and there was a peculiar sickly, smoky haze in the room. Aulic was standing by his side, a look of nervous satisfaction on his wizened face.

The twins watched apprehensively from the passage.

Their father turned and said to them sternly, "Close the door. What I have to say to these two is not for your ears."

Cassie began to protest.

"Do as I say," he demanded in a voice she did not dare disobey. They closed the door behind him.

For a minute they listened to the men's voices anxiously.

"Look, Cass, I don't like this," Keiron said. "I'm going to get some help." He ran off.

Cassie listened fearfully at the door, her heart thudding fast, her ears straining to hear what they were saying. Voices became raised and heated. She wondered what she should do if her father was attacked. *Hurry up, Keiron*, she whispered to herself.

But Keiron was having difficulties. Most of the wolf-people had already left the Mansion and the few that remained were on the point of leaving. He found Tara still in the courtyard, alone now in human form, and he explained to her what was happening. She managed to persuade a few of the wolf-people to delay their departure and help Keiron. Together, they ran back into the house.

They found the door open and Cassie bending over her father. He was slumped on the floor, his stick lying ineffectually to one side.

"I have great respect for your father," Badrur was saying, "but he should not have tried to use that stick on me. Take him away."

Tancred groaned.

"What have you done to him?" Keiron shouted; but Badrur only laughed at him.

Keiron looked into the prince's cruel face and he knew then, with a spasm of bitterness, that he had no choice but to help the prince find the Helmet. His father's life was at stake.

You shouldn't help him, said Will fiercely.

I know that. But have you any other suggestions?

Will was silent.

The wolf-people carried Lord Tancred back to his bed.

"He is so weak," said Cassie, staring into his sleeping face. "Aulic has done his work well."

"You stay with him," said Keiron. "Keep watch over him. I'm sure these wolf-people will stay and help you. Tara will explain to them what has happened, won't you, Tara?"

She nodded.

Keiron steeled himself to return to Prince Badrur.

The room was even more hazy with scented fumes. When Keiron came in Aulic sneered and began to dance around him gleefully. "Your days of ordering me about are over," he sneered. "Now you'll do as we say, you insolent little dog."

Keiron glowered but tried to keep his cool.

"Well?" said Badrur. "What's it to be?"

"My father needs his medicine. Let me have it and then I'll do my best to help you find the Helmet."

Badrur shook his head and took another puff on his hookah. "The Helmet first."

"The Helmet first," Aulic echoed gleefully.

Keiron had no choice. He sighed wearily. He had been puzzling in vain about what Magda could have meant about the Helmet being buried with the dead.

He began his search directly outside Badrur's room. *Tapestry, do you know which way lies the Golden Helmet of the legend?*

He was not surprised by the answer. *I have hung here for more years than I can count, but no whisper of that has passed through my threads.*

126

Prince Badrur, following closely behind, said impatiently, "Well?"

"The tapestry does not know."

"Then ask something else, idiot," said Aulic.

Keiron went down the passage. He touched a carved wooden chest. *Do you know where the Helmet is?*

I am older than the tapestry, but no notion of that has dusted my carvings.

Similar unhelpful answers came from a spear on the wall, an ancient pot in an alcove, even a heraldic carving in the arch over the foot of the stairs, just as he expected.

"We are wasting our time!" Aulic suddenly exclaimed, hitting the palm of his hand against his brow. "Of course! Why didn't I think of it?"

"Think of what?" Badrur demanded.

"The crypt beneath the Chapel. That's where we should be looking."

Keiron's heart sank.

I think he's on to it, said Will. *Now we are for it!*

"Is it there?" Badrur said, grasping hold of the boy's hair and shaking him angrily.

"I don't know of any crypt," Keiron protested. "I don't know what he's talking about."

Badrur glanced at Aulic for confirmation of this. Aulic shrugged his shoulders, as if to say, Why should he know?

They hurried down to the Chapel. Aulic pushed Keiron along in front of him.

Access to the crypt was through a flagstone to the left of the altar. It looked no different from the other flagstones, and there was no indication that there was anything but the foundations beneath it. It took the two men to lift the great slab. Darkness and coldness emanated from the vault and Keiron shivered at the prospect of going down it. Aulic went to fetch lamps.

While they were waiting, Badrur looked about the Chapel contemptuously. Soon, all this would be his. What would he do with this building? He didn't really believe in gods, only in personal magic. Perhaps this could be a kind of throne room, something to match his mother's on East Island.

Keiron watched him warily. Now that there was a real prospect of finding the Helmet, he was more afraid than ever. Finding courage, he asked the prince, "What will you do with the Helmet if we find it?"

A look of cold delight passed over Badrur's face. "I shall make this an island of ice and snow, to match my dreams."

Keiron tried not to flinch. "But you've got to unlock the magic in it first."

He shrugged as if this was a small matter. "And that will only be the start. If I can find the Helmet, then why not the other pieces of the Golden Armour? They are indestructible – why shouldn't I find them and take the Armour's power for myself?"

"Will you let my father, Cassie and I go? We'd be no more trouble. We'd keep out of your way."

"It depends on your magic," he said. "If it can be of use to me. If not, well..." and he shrugged his shoulders.

Aulic returned with the lamps. They each took one and descended the steps into the chill gloom of the crypt. Moving along a low passage, they entered a large chamber. Vermin scuttled out of the lamplight, and giant spiders watched them from nets and hammocks of thick dusty webs. In this chamber were stacked stone coffins. Addressing these, Keiron said, *Does any one of you hold the goddess Citatha's Golden Helmet?*

For a moment there was a deep silence, then an icy chill curled up inside the boy and he began to shake. A voice like a concentrated wheeze stirred from the stone and spoke in elongated syllables that made it hard for the boy to understand. But he made out, *Only the evil or the desperate would summon us from our ancient sleep. Which are you?*

Desperate!

Yet with so much power? We know of no other who can talk to the dead.

I am with someone who has a power over me. I ask at his bidding.

Ah! And why does he wish to know of the Golden Helmet?

He wants its power. He wants to use it to hypnotize and freeze the whole island.

Then why are you helping him?

I have no choice. He will kill me. Please help me.

All I will tell you is that the Helmet is not in the coffins down here.

Keiron closed his eyes tightly and the lamp shook in his hand. He had felt so sure. . . *Am I near it?*

It is among the dead.

Where?

But there was no further answer.

"It's here somewhere," Keiron said to the two men, who had been waiting impatiently. "But the coffin won't say where. Let's move on."

They passed from the chamber of coffins into another where the air was even more chill and dank. Keiron, shivering, held up his lamp. What he saw made him want to turn tail and run, but Badrur put a restraining hand on his shoulder. Before them were row upon row of skulls stacked at crazy angles and covered in a grey film of dust. Their eye sockets stared back sightless and their yellowed teeth grinned in the flickering lamplight. On a shelf below them were the rest of the bones, a great tangled mass of them.

Badrur could feel the boy trembling violently. "You shouldn't be afraid of them," he said, chuckling. "After all, I imagine they are your relatives. It's about time you paid them a visit. Some of them must be the bones of boys like you, felled by some accident or disease. Terrible thought, isn't it?"

Goaded by Badrur's sarcasm, Keiron felt like swinging his fist round and thumping it into the prince's midriff. He quelled the impulse, but it gave him a little surge of energy that helped him to face the ordeal.

"Fetch a skull," Badrur ordered Aulic, who had been hanging back, hardly able to look at the mound of staring eye sockets.

Aulic pulled one away, dislodging several others. They fell and fractured like broken eggs around him, making him shout and dance about as if scalded.

"Give that to me," Badrur said, snatching the skull. He held it out to Keiron. "I think this might tell us where the Helmet is, don't you?"

It was a warning that his time was short, and Keiron

took the skull with trembling hands. He put his lamp at his feet and then held the skull at eye-height. *Can you tell us if the Golden Helmet is down here?*

The skull seemed to waver in his hands and Keiron got the impression that it was trying to smile. His question had amused it!

It has made all our timeless dreams pleasant ones.

Then it's here, then?

It is near.

Yes, but it is here? Keiron felt he could scream in frustration: why didn't they give him a clear answer?

When things die, and only their bones remain, who is going to take any interest in them? Death is a good disguise.

Please help me.

But after that, all that Keiron could hear in his head were numerous sighs like a thousand little winds whispering through a ruin.

"It says the Helmet is disguised," said Keiron, interpreting as best he could.

Badrur looked eagerly at the skulls. "Somewhere, among this lot, is the Helmet?"

Keiron shrugged nervously. "It wasn't clear, but..."

"Aulic, you start on the right," Badrur ordered. "And you, boy, on the left. I shall start in the middle." He put down his lamp and scooped up several skulls, some of which fell and smashed. "Come on, it's bound to be here somewhere."

Keiron picked up each dusty skull in turn, trying not to remember that it was once someone's head. He felt the dark sockets were watching him and he continued to hear their sighs and moans, like currents through the underground chambers. He worked his way methodically through the pile, placing each skull carefully on the ground to one side.

After an initial frenzy, the other two had calmed down and were working swiftly, Aulic swearing softly to himself, Badrur silent and efficient.

Keiron worked his way down towards the last skull at the back of the shelf. *What will happen if we don't find the Helmet?*

What will happen if we do? said Will.

They came to the last skull; it splintered in Badrur's crushing hands.

He looked livid. "Where is it? he shouted at Keiron. *"Where is it?"*

Keiron cowered. "They won't tell me," he whimpered.

Badrur hit him around the head, sending him sprawling into the bed of broken skulls. "Then you'll stay here until they do tell you," he said.

The two men disappeared before Keiron understood what was happening. He heard the crypt door slam, booming through the darkness.

They've locked us in here, he said to Will, horrified.

Seems like it, said Will. *Glad to see the back of them.*

Keiron peered into the flickering gloom. Luckily, they had left him his lamp. But how long would it be before it went out and plunged him into darkness?

Badrur had not given up. He slammed the door of the crypt, saying, "It must be here somewhere. Search the Chapel."

"But we've searched it a dozen times before," Aulic protested.

"Do it!" Badrur shouted through clenched teeth.

They searched.

When nothing was found, Badrur leaned against the stone altar, intensely frustrated. He stared into its black, polished surface, thinking hard. Gradually, he became aware of his own dark reflection. It was like a shadow. It made him shiver; he thought: *the shadow of death.*

"This altar," he said to Aulic. "Has it ever been lifted?"

Aulic recoiled in horror.

"Then don't you think we ought to?" he said icily. "After all, it might be a tomb."

"It would take ten men to lift that," Aulic said.

"Then fetch my men. Move!"

When Aulic had gone, Badrur stretched his arms over the cold stone. "This is it," he said to himself. "This *must* be it."

The men came, some with bits of iron that could be used as levers. They surrounded the altar and tried to lift the stone slab. It would not give. Levers were inserted, pressure applied... All at once, there was a terrific crack, and the stone split into several jagged pieces. They pulled these aside.

In the coffin-shaped space was a body wrapped in cloth. The cloth crumbled to dust when they touched it. The remains of a skeleton appeared. Where the head should be was a helmet. The Golden Helmet. The dust made it resemble a large skull. The darkness in the visor stared out at them all.

The men drew back in sudden awe.

With trembling fingers, Badrur lifted the Helmet from its ancient resting place. The bones, thus disturbed, dissolved like the cloth. He brushed the dust from the Helmet until it gleamed golden and pure in the light. At last – its power would be his!

CHAPTER 12

Badrur gazed and gazed at the Golden Helmet, his hands shaking with a ferocious excitement. All my life, he thought, has been tending towards this moment. He felt the magnetic power inside him rise and burn like a cold blue flame.

When the goddess Citatha made the Golden Armour she had no notion of the evil that lurks like deep sea monsters in the hearts of humans. She believed that the power she invested in the Golden Armour would only be used to magnify good. She could not have foreseen such a one as Prince Badrur, who would use its power to blight and destroy.

Keiron blundered through the dark to the crypt door. In desperation, he ran his hands over it, and to his joy he discovered that at its base the wood was crumbling with dry rot. It didn't take more than a few minutes for him to gouge a hole, using a shard of skull, big enough for Will to wriggle through it. *The key is still in the lock*, Will said excitedly, and the manikin began to climb up the rusty studs in the door.

A few minutes later Keiron crept up the crypt stairs. He was seen by some of the men, but all their eyes were watching the Helmet glittering in Badrur's hands; no one cared about him any more.

Badrur stood before the shattered altar with the Helmet raised above his head. He paused to savour the moment of triumph.

Keiron shuddered. If the Helmet worked... What then? What evil would the prince unleash in their island? Suddenly he couldn't bear it any more. The terror he had held for so long in check during the search for the Helmet overwhelmed him.

He ran into the passage and crashed against a side-door that led outside. Air, light, space... Gasping in panic, he fumbled with the key. He burst outside and drew in great drafts of cold air.

At the same moment, inside the Chapel, Prince Badrur slowly lowered the Golden Helmet on to his head. He snapped down the visor.

He saw in his mind great snowy wastes – the opposite of all he had been brought up with on East Island; and he willed it. Frost began to spread like an unseen mist over the Chapel, ghostly in the blue light; and the breath of the spectators curled like spectres in the air.

It spread with an amazing rapidity – over the Mansion, over the woods and fields, glittering on the hills, and beyond. Spears of ice formed on the eaves and window-sills. Rivers and lakes froze into sheets of grey ice and waterfalls into twisted sculptures. Trees became so laden with freezing rain their boughs began to crack and break.

The Golden Helmet was at last revealing the nature of its magic. It took what was in the heart, the mind, the soul of its wearer and radiated it over the whole land.

Insects, birds and small creatures began to die. Wolves, wild cats, bears, snow-leopards, elks, all the warm-blooded mammals, feeling the full blast of the icy wind, huddled together or scrabbled vainly for their sheltering places, their life blood cooling, their hearts in shock.

Magda, with her prophetic vision, had sensed the approach of this catastrophe. She had got the wolf-people to build great fires outside her caves. They crouched around the flames, anxious that the fires would last long enough to preserve their lives.

In the villages the people looked aghast at the sky, and felt the chill wind seep into their bones.

Cassie, Tara and Lord Tancred huddled together in Tancred's great bed, bemused by the biting chill that cut through their clothes and turned their breath into clouds of freezing mist. Terror struck the children, and Tancred shivered in an astounded daze.

Gradually, the cold deepened and the island turned into a raging blizzard.

Only the monstrous child that Cassie had brought alive seemed unaffected by the change. She, far away in the woods, scooped up the snow and lumbered about in a strange dance among the whirling snowflakes, shrieking with delight.

The prince himself felt the chill strike in his head and travel down to his chest. At first he did not care. He was full of exaltation. The Helmet showed him what was happening all over the island. The ice in his soul was being magnified a thousandfold.

He saw Aulic stagger out of the Chapel. He was aware of his men collapsing on their knees, frost on their eyelids and in their hair, but he no longer cared about them.

He wanted to see, to feel, to exalt over, the effect of his power for himself.

Walking from the Chapel, he came to the side door which Keiron had unlocked. He saw that the boy had collapsed by a tree. He laughed softly to himself and made no effort to rescue him – what need did he have of the boy's puny powers now? He took in the great, magnificent white sweep of the world, thick with swirling snow: here was the measure of his power.

But the cold was now too uncomfortable even for him. He placed his hands either side of the Helmet and tried to lift it. To his surprise, it would not move. He tugged and tugged at it. It held fast. In panic, he pulled so hard he was in danger of breaking his jaw.

Staggering back inside the Chapel, he writhed in a frenzy to wrench the Helmet off. He fell to his knees, the cold weakening his limbs. "Let me go!" he bellowed. The Helmet clung on, as if it wanted to punish him.

Outside, the snow thickened.

Wake up, Keiron. Wake up. Oh, do wake up, Will shouted again and again. He pulled at Keiron's jerkin, at the boy's ears, his hair, his nose, shouting all the while, *Wake up! Wake up!*

Keiron stirred. He flicked open his frost-rimed eyelid. *What's happening. . . ? Let me sleep.*

Will hugged the boy's left ear. *Not when my sap starts freezing, you don't,* he said. *You must wake up.* In desperation, he sunk his sharp little teeth into Will's earlobe. In his extreme numbness, Keiron hardly felt it, but it was enough to make the boy open his eyes again and this time register what was happening.

With difficulty, for his limbs had all but frozen into immobility, he made his way slowly into the Mansion. He locked the door to the main building behind him, aware that Badrur's men were staggering bewildered from the Chapel, his fingers almost too numb to turn the key. He climbed the stairs, slowly and painfully, and Will had to urge him on at almost every step.

He found his father, Cassie and Tara still trembling under furs and blankets on the bed. He was so dazed with cold he hardly knew what he was doing, but he blurted out, "Badrur! He's got the Helmet. He's turning us all into ice." He collapsed in front of the fire.

His words had an electric effect on Cassie. She untangled herself from the others and climbed out of the bed. The cold enveloped her. She seized one of her father's robes, feeling the chill air at every breath rasping in her chest, and threw it over her brother.

"Is he all right?" her father asked, struggling to get up.

"He's very cold, almost blue," she said.

Tara came over to them and lay down beside him. "We'll warm him," she said, and both girls covered him with their warmth.

They felt his shivering slowly pass. Colour came back into his face. Eventually, he sat up. In a confused voice, he told them what had happened. "You must get the Helmet off him. It's him that's causing the great freeze. Hurry!"

The girls pulled on furs and ran through the freezing house, clouds of cold breath wafting behind them. There was no sign of anyone either inside or outside and the silence of the place struck them both as eerie, unnatural. Outside, the wind swept through broken trees and over the whitened landscape, throwing sleet against the window panes.

They unlocked the door and flitted down the passage, into the Chapel.

Prince Badrur was still lying there, unconscious. They stared at him, too afraid to approach for a while.

"We must get it off," said Cassie, pointing at the Helmet.

It glimmered softly in the ghostly light.

They knelt either side of the Helmet and saw their faces reflected in the gold. "I can't believe I'm looking at it," Cassie said breathlessly, her eyes glittering.

"He brought the snow, didn't he?" Tara said, understanding for the first time what had happened.

"He and the Helmet," Cassie said with awe.

In the fall, the Helmet had tilted slightly to one side, and this seemed to have loosened it. It resisted their efforts for a while, then suddenly came off, making them both fall back. It rolled a few feet away and rocked for a while.

"Is he dead?" Cassie wondered, looking down at the unconscious prince.

"I hope so," said Tara, suddenly baring her teeth as if she was a wolf. "Come on, let's leave him."

As they ran from the Chapel, Cassie held the Helmet up before her like a banner. She felt the warmth of the gold, and she fancied she could see a green light glowing inside it.

All night Lord Tancred, wrapped in furs before a fire, held the Helmet in his hands, admiring it, polishing it, dreaming over it. This unexpected culmination of his lifetime's search for it filled him with such joy, his illness fell away from him. He fancied he could feel some inner vibration in it which was subtly transforming him.

Nearby, his children and the wolf-girl slept under furs. They had stayed awake for as long as they could, talking excitedly of the Helmet. Cassie had asked her father if she should put the Helmet on. They had all seen how its magic worked, and Cassie knew in her bones that it was her destiny to right what Badrur had done. She had seen, from the roof of the Ice Castle, a vision of the island as a paradise, and she had carried that vision in her heart ever since. The Helmet, she now realized, could make that happen, and she had made her father understand this before, exhausted, she fell asleep.

Tancred checked that the Mansion was secure, then he went down to the Chapel. He stood over the body of Badrur for a long while, wondering whether to revive him or to make sure he was dead. In the end, he dragged the prince out of the Chapel and locked him out in the snow. Let fate decide whether Badrur lived or died.

He spent some of the long hours of the night consulting books on the subject of the Helmet, determined to make sure that his daughter would not be put in any danger.

At dawn, he thought he heard, faintly, the sound of the Mansion gates creaking open. He rubbed the frozen window-pane and peered out. Aulic and a couple of rough-looking men were spurring on horses in the snow. He looked closer: one of the horses seemed riderless, unless that was a body slung across it. Badrur! So he was still unconscious. Or dead; he hoped so. He hoped they would all perish in the snow; it was what they deserved.

Later that morning, the four of them gathered in the Chapel.

Cassie's father placed the Golden Helmet in his daughter's hands. "You are right, Cassie, I feel sure of it now. You are destined to use your life-giving powers to save this island," he told her solemnly. "We now know that once the Helmet is placed over the head, it magnifies a thousandfold and more what is in the wearer's heart."

So this was it: what she had always dreamed of. But now, instead of creating a paradise, she first had to undo all Badrur's work. With shaking hands, she lifted the Helmet and lowered it apprehensively over her head.

She felt a great outflowing of energy and warmth, drawn from a deep unfathomable source within her. She saw a sun blaze over the island. In a moving panorama before her eyes, she saw sunlight glitter on the quilt of snow over the island. Layers of frost melted from walls and branches. Waterfalls cracked and shattered and gushed forth again. Animals and birds, as if brought back from the dead, lifted their heads and stretched their wings. The sky cleared rapidly of its grey pall and a crystal blue arched over everything. Snow trickled away in tiny little glittering streams. Sunlight intensified, glanced off every melting surface, healed frostbite and loosened shrivelled buds.

In Magda's cave, the wolf-people yapped in relief and the old woman murmured a prayer of thanks.

Villagers and trappers came out of their huts, held up their faces and hands to the light and heat, and listened with amazement to a world without a taunting wind. They danced about in disbelief, crying and laughing.

When the great thaw reached the northernmost tips of the island, the warmth even made its way into the Ice Castle and raised Angharer from what she thought was her deathbed. She looked out over the island from the roof of the castle and wondered at the way stunted trees were turning green and the land seemed suddenly bursting with life.

Then slowly the light inside Cassie began to dim. If she had not had to undo Badrur's icy grip on the island, the warmth from her heart would have been more than enough to transform it for good; but that was not to be. She was not aware of that, not yet. She felt an immense tiredness steal through her. With some effort, she lifted the Helmet from her head and handed it back with trembling hands to her father.

"Are you all right, Cass?" Keiron asked. "You look so white."

She smiled weakly, and then yawned. "I'm happy," she said. "I've done what I've always dreamt of doing. But it's really taken it out of me."

Attracted by the sunlight, they paused at the door in the passage.

"It's so quiet," said Tara. "And so beautiful."

"It's brilliant," said Keiron, holding up his hands and dancing about. "You've brought the island back to life, Cass. You've given us sunlight, just like you said you always wanted to."

"Not I," said Cassie, waving a self-deprecating hand. "The Helmet."

"It only magnified what was in you."

They shed their coats and outer clothing and lingered in the sunlight, marvelling at how warm it felt on their skin.

Tancred sat at his desk, turning and turning the Helmet in front of him. He lifted it once or twice and held it above his head, but being a man without vanity or impulse, he had the sense not to put it on and confuse everyone and every being with the perplexed tangle of his thoughts. But the thing was a wonder, so dignified and hypnotic in its ancient silence and hidden power. He was immensely proud of his daughter, proud to think that it was she, out of all the generations of his family, who had the transforming power in her heart, made powerful by this Helmet. But he could see how much the effort had cost her.

While Cassie sat dreamily by the fire, Tara and Keiron went down into the kitchens to prepare the dinner, and they made a great and cheerful mess.

"Not too bad," said Lord Tancred, valiantly chewing his way through a plate of steaming elk stew. "But I think we'll have to hire some villagers to do the cooking in future, don't you?"

Tara giggled and nodded.

What a day, said Keiron as he wriggled into bed that night.

Not one I'd wish to repeat, said Will, settling to sleep in the boy's uncombed hair. *Despite all that sap rising. It won't last, you know.*

What?

I can feel it. It's like a false spring.

Oh, come on, Will! Don't be so doomy!

Will refused to dignify that with a reply.

Keiron closed his eyes. He had a flashback of himself collapsing in the snow by the tree, succumbing to the ruthless cold; the flame of his life flickered so low one puff might have snuffed it out.

I didn't thank you for biting my ear, Will.

No, you didn't.

Well, I just don't want you to make a habit of it, all right?

In her bedroom, Cassie threw off a couple of blankets. "I've never known it so warm as this," she said with a laugh.

"Are you glad that Badrur found the Helmet?"

"Of course," said Cassie; but as she lay there, she wondered about that. It had freed her father from his illness, and it had transformed the island, but on the other hand, it had nearly caused Keiron's death. "Of course," she murmured again, less sure this time.

145

"Good night, Tara," she whispered sleepily. "Better times are ahead. We can go on picnics."

"Picnics?" Tara answered. "What are they?"

For three days they enjoyed the sunshine, the silence filled only with birdsong and the hum of insects, the sense of peace, or respite, that bathed the Mansion. But all this time unseen forces of nature were in conflict.

On the third night, Cassie woke from a troubled sleep. She sat up, and with a sinking heart, she knew what had woken her: *the wind was howling again!* Just as it always had done, angry and contemptuous.

She opened the window and saw, in the scudding moonlight, that the harsh climate of the island was beginning to return. Trees bent under the lash of a hailstorm and a cold wind whipped round her body. It was as they had all feared: the sunshine had been only a brief respite, enough to get rid of Badrur's great freeze but not enough to turn it for ever into the land of gentle sunlight and rain that she had always wanted. Bitterly, she brooded on that until the thought was like a torture.

Tara was sitting up listening to the wind with dismay too. Cassie told the wolf-girl what she thought she ought to do. Tara felt uneasy about it but as Cassie was determined, she kept her feelings to herself.

They crept to Lord Tancred's room. There the Helmet gleamed in the moonlight on his desk.

She sat in her father's chair. "Should we do it?" she whispered. The Helmet was so awesome: it had a faint glow around it, and its visor stared at her implacably. It did not like its power to be taken for granted. But surely she had to finish her work, realize her dream? The Helmet would understand that.

With shaking hands, she lifted the Helmet and lowered it over her head. Whereas before, it radiated light, now it seemed to intensify the night around her. Suddenly she was alone in an infinity of dark space. In a panic, she tried to lift the helmet off, but it would not budge.

She calmed her fears then, and concentrated her mind. She thought of life, the life-giving force, like an eternal sap running through the land. She thought of flowers opening, buds unfurling, water flowing...

But, terrifyingly, the images that came back to her, crowding out her own, were of night creatures swivelling their heads to watch her, their startled eyes flicking open. Owls and night-vultures, horned pigs and toads with flicking tongues, prowling wild cats that hissed and snarled: they seemed to grow larger and stronger before her eyes. She sent out a message, *No, that's not what I mean. Something deeper, something older that will change the island for good.*

In the daytime, such words would have harnessed sunlight. But her power was appealing to the night world. As she concentrated, the Helmet radiated life deep into older, darker, harder things, into rock, into petrified statues. The rock did not matter, for it had never lived, but all the hideous creatures that had been fossilized in dark magic ages ago around the Ice Castle felt the Helmet's power stir their being.

Snow melted from the creatures. They moved, stiff and jerky. Crusts of moss and growth cracked and fell away from them. Eye sockets glowed blood-red, green and amber. Membranes pulsed. Wings flapped, talons emerged, claws swiped the air, jaws opened and rumbling bellows boomed through the night. Huge beetles broke from their stone prisons. Lumbering beasts without a name lifted heavy feet and thumped them on the earth. Stone beings were rising into dark and terrifying life.

Cassie gasped. In her mind, she saw the great salamander by the castle walls turn its scaly head and glare hatefully at her. Its eyes were like a dark green slimy pool into which all life would be sucked and drowned.

She screamed.

Tara wrenched so hard on the Helmet, it shifted its angle. That was enough to disturb the flow of energy. Cassie lent her hands to it and together they wrenched it off.

But it was too late. The ancient beasts around the Ice Castle had been roused from their deep slumber.

Cassie clutched the wolf-girl. "What have I done?" she whispered. "What have I done?"

CHAPTER 13

Magda and her wolf-people woke with a start in their caves. They heard cries and shrieks in the forest and wondered what could be disturbing the night creatures. The medicine woman listened, and after a lull in the stirring, she cried out in horror, "She is waking the dead. The monsters of stone. Does she not realize...? Oh, but she must stop. I feel their cold blood pulsing..."

The wolf-people crowded about her in alarm. They watched as she shook and gibbered, intense fear in her face. Then she went limp and sunk to her knees. "She has stopped it," she whispered. "But the damage is done." For a moment she was paralysed with indecision. She poured herself some dark liquid from a cauldron and gulped it down.

She spoke to the wolf-people at her cave entrance. "You must go to the villages and warn them that the stone monsters have been brought to life. They must do all they can to avoid them and resist them – as we must, too. Go, and do your best."

The wolf-people streamed out into the island.

*　*　*

On their way back to the Ice Castle, Badrur, who had been unconscious for days, came to with a sudden jerk of his body, and sat up on his horse. He was all for galloping back and wresting the Helmet from Tancred, but Aulic was of the opinion that the wolf-people would be guarding the Mansion by now, called to defend the ruling family. It was late, too, and the Mansion was several days' ride away.

They stopped off at a village and demanded food. At first the village elder was inclined to refuse them – until Badrur, with one long sweep of his dark, fiery eyes, hypnotized their hunting dogs and threatened to set them on their owners.

After the meal he decided to stay for the night. He kicked Aulic out of the hut he had commandeered, set a ring of obedient dogs around it, and settled down to plan his next moves. Before, the seizure of the Mansion and the disposal of the ruling family had been a pleasant idea to be executed when the time was right; now, revenge smouldered in him. He would wipe them out for good and rule over the island, bend the villagers and wolf-people to his will, make them all shiver in perpetual snow; he would set up a new seat of power... It was only a matter of time.

He rose at first light. The villagers were still sleeping. To stretch his legs, he strolled out of the clearing and into the surrounding wood. It was full of rustling sounds, of creatures moving about just beyond his vision, and he wondered why it should be so noisy here.

Further on, he came to a stream. He removed his clothes and bathed in the icy waters.

Sitting on a rock to let the wind dry him, he became conscious of a crashing sound, loud and rhythmic, like the tread of a heavy animal. He rose to fetch his clothes, but he didn't get far.

Emerging from the trees was a giant infant. Naked and streaked with mud, she was half as tall as him, like a giant's offspring. He recognized the baby he'd seen before, the one that that strange child Cassie had brought back from the dead. What incredible growth! He could hardly believe his eyes.

Few things made Prince Badrur afraid, but this child did, and he did not know why. He watched helplessly as the child lumbered up to him, gurgling with pleasure. She splashed into the water and threw her arms around him. She slobbered kisses and dribbled over him until he found the strength to wriggle out of her grasp in disgust.

For a few brief seconds she had looked into his eyes and saw the wastes of snow there, strengthening the dark, destructive bond which had begun to form between them.

He scrambled frantically for his clothes and ran from the river.

Distraught, she followed him, calling out in bewilderment; and then, as he disappeared, she cried in frustration. She was like an abandoned child looking for her parents. In her mind was a vague, fading image of the girl, the first to look into her eyes: surely that had been her mother? And now this one. Was he her father?

In the village, Badrur leapt on to his horse and galloped off without a word. Aulic scrambled after him.

A few minutes later, the Child, as she came to be known, pounded into the village. When she understood that Badrur had fled, she grew angry and began to stomp around, flailing her arms, kicking at what was in her path, bawling.

The villagers set the dogs on her, then recoiled in amazement. Each dog she touched fell dead. And at each death she seemed to grow a fraction, as if she was feeding off their life-force.

The villagers scattered into the forest and watched in horror as she pushed down wooden huts, trampled on food crops, frightened livestock. They were terrified: who was this monstrous child with the strength of ten men and the touch of death?

Some of the villagers began to hurl knives and stones and arrows at her. That was futile too: there seemed some kind of aura around her, an invisible shield which deflected the missiles. She hardly noticed them. The villagers knew then that they were in the presence of a creature protected by some dark god, and they fled into the forest.

Prince Badrur rode steadily for the next few days, leaving Aulic to trail wearily in his wake, until he drew near the Ice Castle.

He knew something strange had occurred here. There were signs of destruction everywhere: broken trees, trampled bushes, trappers' huts smashed, dead animals. He came across the body of one of his men, torn to pieces and half eaten. It wasn't long before he came face to face with the cause. A great shadow fell over him. Looking up, he saw a huge birdlike creature with a great beak. He could hear the creak of its wings. It suddenly dive-bombed him and he only just got out of its path in time. It landed on a rock and stared at him. He recognized it as one of the petrified creatures of the Ice Castle and guessed at once what had happened. The Golden Helmet had brought them alive! He laughed at that, a sudden joy in his heart. The creature hopped down from the rock and bounded towards him. His horse shied up in a panic and he had to dismount. He stood boldly in the path of the creature. One look into his hypnotic eye and the creature was helpless.

"You are mine now," Badrur said to it. "Go back to the castle and tell them I am coming."

The giant bird ran forward submissively, flapped its creaking wings, and took off.

Badrur slowed his pace after that, curious to see what other creatures he might encounter. He was not disappointed. What he took to be a large, smoothly rounded rock by the trackside suddenly moved as he approached, and with a hiss its domed shell opened, revealing a bristle of steel-like fins. From a tree above, a lizard-like creature flicked out a poisonous tongue, and two huge spiders were spinning a cocoon around a writhing bird.

Such sights excited him; and as he progressed, he spun his own hypnotic web. By the time he reached the castle, he had a small army of shuffling, hopping, leaping, lumbering and flying creatures in his wake, ready to do his bidding.

He found the main castle gates smashed.

His horse would go no further, and he dismounted. A couple of his men appeared around the side of the castle but on seeing the seething crowd of monsters, they fled before he could speak to them.

In the centre of the courtyard was the giant salamander. It was devouring a horse. Its teeth tore at the flesh, its grey-green scales bloody and glistening. Seeing Badrur, it rose and snorted. It towered over him. Badrur concentrated his power into its blood-rimmed eyes. The beast resisted far longer than any of the other creatures. It was a battle of wills. Badrur stood his ground and stared and stared until he penetrated right to the heart of that ancient and cruel beast. The salamander swayed back and forth. And then its resistance suddenly broke. With a slow sigh, it sunk on all fours and bowed its head before him.

He approached it and touched its head, getting blood on his hands. "You shall be dearer to me than all the creatures," he said solemnly. "For you are nobler than the rest. Once you were king in your land, and you shall be the first among equals here."

To his surprise, the great salamander answered him, a deep, hoarse voice in his head. *You are like that other one that brought us here, when we first came. He had the same power over us. Have you come to take us back home?*

Badrur pondered this. "I have come to make *this* island your home," he said at last. "You and I will rule it."

We are used to deserts. We do not like the cold.

"There are no deserts on this island; you will have to adjust. But it is warmer further south. There's a mansion there where we can live. But first we have to clear it of its present inhabitants, some troublesome humans of no account. And we have to tame the humans of the island and their allies the wolf-people. I fear there will be a messy battle."

There is nothing we would like better.

"Good. Then explain to your fellow creatures that we shall leave tomorrow, all of us, to do what we have to. Anything that resists them must be killed – that's all they need to know."

Badrur found most of his men in the dining-hall. They reported that the creatures had eaten their horses and they feared for their own lives. Angharer was trying to feed them with dwindling supplies. They had all seen how with the Helmet he had turned the island into a snowy waste; they had seen how he had suborned the creatures, and they looked at him now not just with awe but with fear, as one might look upon a capricious god. Even his aunt was a little tremulous as she spoke to him.

The following morning, they all streamed out into the courtyard. There, the Great Salamander had assembled some of the creatures. With acute apprehension, the men, at Badrur's bidding, had to mount them, their horses having been devoured. They balanced precariously on slithery backs, clinging to leathery skins or tough fins, some rising higher than they'd ever been before on any creature.

The Great Salamander lowered its long neck at Badrur's approach and he perched himself on its neck, tucking his feet into some gills and holding on to a kind of ruff at its neck.

Angharer stood on the roof to watch this ugly and outlandish army make its way out of the coutyard, and join the rest of the creatures waiting outside. She looked with pride at her foster-child riding so magnificently at the head of it, held high on the monster's neck. On his return, she told herself, he would be ruler of North Island and she would be like a dowager queen. It was no less than he had promised.

In the days ahead visitors came to see Lord Tancred, with tales of strange sightings, of outlandish flying creatures in the sky, of savaged dogs and horses, of terrified trappers who spoke of a great nightmare army approaching the Mansion. Cassie had not dared tell him of the awakening of the beasts – for a long time, she denied even to herself that she had done it, hoping it was an illusion, like a nightmare – and he was puzzled. Was this the work of the Helmet too? He did not want to believe it. And now that he had no wolf-people to do his bidding, he had no one to send out to find the truth; but when he saw a great dragon-like bird flap slowly over the Mansion, his doubts disappeared.

He said to Keiron, "Come with me, my boy. I've seen and heard enough to know that we must prepare an escape route."

They rode down to the harbour where Lord Tancred's ship was moored, rising proudly above the fishing boats. He seldom used it, but he liked to visit it from time to time and make sure that the hands who looked after it were keeping it in good repair.

Keiron climbed up the rigging and sat in the crow's nest, the wind streaming out his hair and buffeting his ears. Great dark clouds were massing over the sea and a cold rain began to beat viciously on his head: those three days of mild sunshine and calm breezes now seemed a cruel taunt to him.

Faintly, he heard his father give orders that the ship should be put in readiness for sailing, with supplies on board and the sails checked. Looking across the choppy sea, he thought, "Yes, it'd be nice to sail off to a warmer place, a *different* place, where we are not threatened by who knows what. I wonder what Father has in mind?"

What do you think, Will?

I think dreams sometimes come true.

But where would you like to go?

Where you go, I go.

A movement on land caught his eye. He strained to see beyond the Mansion. What was that? It resembled some huge, creeping shadow moving slowly towards the Mansion. Like a motley army.

"Father!" he shouted. He pointed to the ridge and breathlessly tried to explain what he had seen, but half his words were drowned by the drumming of the rain.

When they arrived back at the Mansion, drenched, they were perturbed to see a crowd of villagers and wolf-people massing all about its walls and getting bigger by the minute. Cassie, at an upstairs window with Tara, shouted down to them, "Magda told them to come. She's in the courtyard."

The crowd parted to let them pass and they found the old woman, tall and gaunt among a crowd of silent wolf-people. She looked at Tancred sternly and said, "You must believe it now. By the morrow, we shall be attacked by Prince Badrur's hideous hordes, those monstrous creatures that your daughter, in her great folly, brought alive and whose evil power he has harnessed."

He gave his daughter one half-withering, half-pitying glance. It was the first indication she'd had that he knew, and she blinked back tears of self-reproach.

Magda continued. "We shall all fight them, but what weapons beyond courage do we have against such creatures?"

A ripple of unease passed through the wolf-people. They already sensed the blood that would be shed.

Lord Tancred invited Magda inside to plan tactics. "All we can do is resist," she said. "There is nothing more we can do."

"But can't we dig traps for the creatures?" said Keiron desperately.

"No time," said the woman. "They will attack at daybreak."

Later that evening, Lord Tancred, fired by the supreme test ahead of them all, spoke to the assembled crowd from the battlements. Magda was at his side. "Prince Badrur will try to hypnotize you," Tancred shouted. "Keep your eyes lowered; resist him with all your might; you have held against him before, you will do so again. Don't try and fight the monsters on your own: a crowd of you against each one is more likely to defeat them. Bring them down with your ropes and arrows. Spear their hearts..."

Magda added, "Wolf-people, if he wins, you will all be enslaved. He will rob you of your skins, and you will be enslaved to him. Resist him with all your ferocious and courageous might. Use all the cunning you have learnt on the hunt..."

Tancred insisted that the twins and Tara should spend the night on the ship. It was the least dangerous place and they would be ready to flee should the battle go against them. They knew better than to plead otherwise at such a time, and they were escorted down to the ship and made snug in one of its cabins. Lord Tancred hugged them all and promised that he would see them again "when all this is over".

Cassie was in a fever of self-reproach and apprehension, and the fears of the other two were put aside in their attempts to calm her and talk sense into her. "But I unleashed those monsters," she said again and again.

"You didn't. The Helmet did," they kept replying.

It was a long night. They got little sleep.

At dawn Cassie crept out of the cabin and went up on deck. The sun was just cresting the horizon of the sea. The cold wind pushed her towards the edge of the ship, and for a few seconds she let herself be pushed; but at the edge she grasped a rope and saved herself. She stared down into the dark, swelling sea. Yes, she thought grimly, I deserve to fall and sink into that after what I have done.

The brief, struggling sunlight played on her hair and she looked up. The crow's nest! She climbed the rigging and settled into the high and lonely look-out. On one side stretched the sea and the promise of other lands. On the other... She looked at her home with hate and shame. Why had the goddess Citatha created such a flawed, such a dangerous suit of armour? Couldn't she have done something else?

She closed her eyes and a vision of the Golden Armour in the temple vault came to her, vivid and mysterious. The wind dropped and turned to a whisper, and that whisper turned into words: *Forgive me. I did not know my subjects. You must take the Helmet back to Temple Island. It will be safe only when it is reunited with the Golden Armour. I shall watch over you.*

At once, Cassie felt the burden of guilt fall away from her and her heart lighten. She knew the voice was more than her own thoughts, but she dared not ask who spoke it. It was all part of the battle that was about to be fought – had to be fought. She shinned down the rigging to rouse her brother and Tara.

Keiron was already on deck, staring across at the outline of the Mansion.

"Cass," he said, a look of sullen determination on his face. "I can't stay here while all of them, the wolf-people and the villagers, even Magda, are fighting for us. It isn't fair. You stay here with Tara if you want to – I shan't blame you if you do – but I'm going back, Father or no Father."

"I'm coming too, then," she answered. "Don't you think I feel the same?"

"I was going anyway," said Tara, who had appeared silently beside them. "My people are fighting there. I must be with them."

They slipped off the boat while the crew still slept and ran back towards the Mansion.

As they approached it, they heard an ominous rumbling sound and felt the earth shake. They faltered.

Tara looked more frightened than the other two. "Go back to the ship, Tara," Cassie urged. "You don't have to face this."

But Tara had a sense that she was going towards her destiny and that she had no choice in the matter. "I have to," she said simply.

She pointed towards the ridge. "Look!" she cried. The first of Badrur's terrible army appeared, cut black against the grey sky. Stone monsters, now livid in the early sunlight, massed along the ridge. In the middle of them appeared the prince. He reared up on his giant mount. The Great Salamander roared, a deep boom echoing across the valley to the Mansion and beyond.

CHAPTER 14

The children joined Lord Tancred and Magda on the battlemented roof. For a few minutes Tancred was furious with them for disobeying him and was ordering them back to the boat when Magda, who could see how much the children wanted to be involved, put her hand on his arm and said, "It will help our side to see the children here. It will remind them of who and what they are fighting for. If the battle goes against us, you will know in good time and can still make your escape. Let them stay."

She prevailed, and the three children took up their positions overlooking the expanse of land, studded with small trees and bushes, in front of the Mansion where the battle would be fought.

But they were not able to stay there for long. Out of the sky came hideous birds with giant wing-spans, vicious talons, deadly beaks. They swooped down on to the roof. One wolf-woman, taken by surprise, was seized by three of them and torn apart before their eyes. The twins turned away, feeling sick to the pit of their stomachs, but Tara stared in horror. They fled as quickly as they could, closing the trapdoor behind them just in time. It was a foretaste of what was to come.

"Fetch us some weapons," Tancred ordered a wolf-man who had recently served in the Mansion.

The twins had their pick of bows and arrows, daggers, swords, slings and spears; they each seized a bow and arrows. Tara looked at the weapons scornfully.

"Go on," Cassie urged. "You might need one."

The wolf-girl shook her head. "Wolf-people have never fought with man's weapons," she said. "And when I go out there..."

"You're not going out there?" Keiron butted in. "It's too dangerous. We shall fight from the Mansion."

"I might have to," said Tara, "and when I do, I shall become a wolf again." There was a glint of seriousness, of gravity, in her eye which Cassie did not remember having seen before.

The stone monsters had reached the foot of the ridge and were now advancing on the Mansion, Badrur's men amongst them. The villagers, the wolf-people, everyone watching from the Mansion, felt as if they were looking into an abyss and seeing nightmares more hideous than even the sleeping mind could conjure.

The heavy beasts made the earth shake, the slithery creatures made the earth hiss, the darting creatures made the earth crack and spatter mud. The flying creatures, including huge, nightmarish insects, sliced up the wind and blotted out the light. The tall, long-necked creatures swayed back and forth, their teeth glinting, their eyes a smouldering red or green.

Prince Badrur kept watch on the ridge, high on the neck of his growling salamander.

Aulic dismounted too, intending to stay out of harm's way, but Badrur threatened to wring his neck if he did not join the battle. Utterly dismayed, and shaking all over, Aulic remounted his armadillo-like creature and shuffled forward. How bitterly he regretted now not staying in hiding.

Lord Tancred sensed a wave of fear pass through his forces. He shouted from the window, "Remember, fight each one of them in groups. Bring them down with your ropes and weapons and pierce their hearts."

Winged monsters descended on the wolf-people. One was caught and slaughtered in a rain of spears. But another seized a wolf-man: for a moment he wriggled in the talons of the bird above them, crying in sheer terror, then he was dropped to the earth, smashing his skull.

The battle had begun.

The monsters had far more destructive power and were harder to kill than their opponents, but they were greatly outnumbered, making this a more even match than it looked. In the bloody hour ahead, filled with fatal intensity, the fortunes of the battle swayed back and forth: it was impossible to tell who was getting the upper hand.

Keiron saw a group of wolf-people seize in their strong jaws the feet and tail of a slithery lizard-like creature which had sharp, knife-like fins down its back. The wolves pulled, the blades slashed ineffectually, the beast bellowed. "Pull harder," Keiron urged, though he could not be heard by them. Several more wolf-people converged on them. They threw what looked like a sack made of fur over the creature's snout. In a few desperate minutes it suffocated. Keiron marvelled at their ingenuity. Magda observed, "That's how we'll win this battle – with cunning, not might."

Cassie was less sure. She had seen three villagers trampled on by a squat creature with huge, plate-like feet. They were helpless against it, for the ruff around its neck seemed to whirr, acting like a shield against their arrows and spears.

A swarm of fat, poisonous-looking insects, as big as puffballs, sailed towards the battlefield, spraying a deadly yellow mist behind them.

Lord Tancred shouted, "Shoot them down." The twins raised their bows and fired arrow after arrow at the flying creatures. The air was so thick with them, most of the arrows found their mark. As each arrow sunk into the fat bodies of the insects, there was a loud hiss and the creature plummeted. But some whirred on unhit, and, enraged, they emitted great clouds of gas that settled on those below, causing screams of pain and confusion.

One of the insects made a beeline for the Mansion. It thudded against the window where, only a moment ago, Tancred was firing his arrows. The creature banged against the leaded glass, its eyes glaring, and then sprayed it with its poison.

The twins felt sick at all this carnage. They tried retreating into the room and not looking, but the suspense was too great. Every time they returned to the window, they focused on some dreadful scene that was like a microcosm of the larger battle.

Keiron watched a great bear-like creature picking off wolves one by one. Its skin was so thick and leathery, arrows and spears just bounced off it, and it was so strong it just scooped up wolves and hurled them into the air. Whatever could they do against that? If such a creature ever got into the Mansion... But some villagers came to the wolves' rescue. They lassoed the creature's arms and head and brought it crashing to the ground. Arrows and spears were fired into its mouth and it writhed in agony, its bellows muffled, until it choked on its own blood. Keiron watched its twitching death throes with horrible fascination.

"We must get the wounded into the Mansion," Magda said. She bustled away, glad to have something to do. Downstairs, she organized teams of wolf-people to go out into the battlefield and bring in the wounded.

Cassie could no longer watch the battle.

"Why don't you go and help Magda?" Tancred said, seeing how pale she looked. "Your healing powers will be put to good use there."

Gratefully, she accepted the idea. She turned to Tara. "Will you come with me?" Together, the two girls ran down to the ground floor.

Keiron passed his father several arrows. "See that crawling thing down there," he shouted above the din, for he had opened the windows again. "I'm sure we could get it from here."

On the ground floor the wounded were being brought into every room. The air was full of their cries of pain. The girls went from one wounded wolf-person or villager to another, giving water, trying to make them more comfortable, saying kind words.

Cassie tentatively touched a deep gash on a woman's brow. The power of healing flowed down her fingers. The wound sealed up without any sign that it had been there. Tara wiped the blood from it and they both stared at the unblemished skin. The woman touched the same spot and said, "It's stopped hurting. Where is it?" She looked bewildered.

Cassie gazed at her hand. She had healed small creatures and little cuts, but there had never been an occasion before to heal deep wounds. What miracle was being worked by her hands! But there was no time to reflect on its power now.

She laid her hand on the smashed leg of a wolf-man and felt a current of healing energy pass through it. She felt the bones and the torn muscles knit together and saw the gashed skin smooth over. The wolf-man's moans ceased and he looked astonished. Then he jumped up from his bed and danced around in delighted disbelief.

Word of Cassie's healing power swept through the improvised wards.

This is the way I can redeem myself, Cassie thought.

Now she went from one wounded person to another, healing each wound. Tara stayed with her, wiping away the blood and dirt. There was a curious mingling of joy and pain. The more she healed, the more the wounded flowed in.

Cassie's miraculous progress faltered when she came across a wolf-boy whose breathing appeared to have stopped. Tara was dismayed to see a wolf-person so young in the battle. She looked closer and recognized him: he was from her own pack, they had played together and learnt to hunt together; they had been friends. "Can't you save him?" she cried in despair at Cassie.

"Is he still alive?" Cassie asked fearfully.

Tara put her head to the wolf-boy's breast. She felt a very faint, slow heartbeat. "Just," Tara cried.

She shook the wolf-boy. He stirred, moaned, opened his eyes. Seeing Tara, he smiled faintly in recognition and whispered her name.

Tara bent very close to him. "Cassie will save you," she said.

A spasm of pain made him arch, and for a while he was speechless. Then he said in a voice she could hardly hear, "They've brought your skin, Tara. In the courtyard..."

Tara stepped back, her eyes wide. *Her skin!* Suddenly, there was nothing in the world she wanted more.

The wolf-boy's head lolled to one side.

Cassie moved forward to lay her hands on him.

"Wait," Tara cried. She pressed her ear against his chest. "His heart's stopped." She tried frantically to bring life back into the boy – thumping his chest, shaking him – but it was no good. All the while she implored Cassie to help her. But Cassie held back. "I cannot bring the dead back to life," she said as Tara wept over the body. "You know what happened last time."

Tara knew, but she wasn't consoled.

She stared at the dead wolf-boy and suddenly she hated herself for hiding here, in her human form, away from the battle, when wolves of her own age were out there fighting for their freedom. That's why he had told her about her skin.

"I must go out there," she said to Cassie.

"No," Cassie protested. "It's too dangerous. You can't."

But nothing would stop Tara now. She ran past the wounded and into the courtyard. There it was! Her skin was draped over the water-butt, the very one she had hid behind on her first day there. She snatched it and with one extraordinary movement of her body, she slid into the skin and became a wolf again.

She padded through the gates and joined the fighting.

Prince Badrur watched impassively from the ridge. He knew that the superior might of his creatures would wear down the resistance eventually; but perhaps there was something he could do to speed matters along. He called to a dragon-like creature gliding overhead. It landed in front of him and folded its wings. "Your snout looks strong," said Badrur. "Is it strong enough to smash through the glass and frame of the Mansion windows?"

By way of demonstration, the dragon-like creature hit a nearby stone with its snout. The stone shattered. The prince was delighted.

"Break into the third window from the left. There you will find Lord Tancred. Tear him to pieces and bring me a mouthful of his flesh."

The dragon-like creature rose and headed straight for the Mansion.

Lord Tancred was still directing the battle – as far as he was able to – from the schoolroom. He saw the approach of the creature. "Look out!" he shouted. He and Keiron jumped back just in time.

There was an explosion of glass and stone. The dragon-like creature crashed on to the floor, knocking aside chairs and splintering globes of the earth and heavens. It got to its feet unscathed and glared at them with angry green eyes. Keiron had never seen anything so terrifying. Its greenish scales glistened, its fangs flared, its veined wings shivered, and a misty stench came from its hot mouth.

Tancred and Keiron backed towards the door.

The creature thumped its snout on the floor. The floorboards splintered. It tossed its snout from side to side, shattering a tall chair that got in its way.

Then it crashed towards them.

They just managed to get through and slam the door. The monster attacked it. As they ran along the corridor, they could hear it smash its way through the door's thick wooden panels.

It blundered into the long passage, smashing everything in its path. It crashed from room to room, as if seeking them out. In Lord Tancred's study it tossed the astrological charts in the air, sent up a cloud of shredded documents, trampled on the books, battered his desk to bits. Below, Tancred listened to the noises; every crash was like a nail in his heart. He knew his life's work was being destroyed and there was nothing he could do about it.

The creature fell silent for a minute.

"Perhaps it's gone," said Keiron hopefully.

By this time there was a crowd of wounded wolf-people and villagers listening to the destruction too.

Their hopes were short-lived. Suddenly, the dragon-like creature was slithering down the stairs, roaring its anger.

At the foot of the stairs the creature observed Tancred and his son, its malevolent eyes burning. Bring back a handful of the old man's flesh, its master had said. Well, it would enjoy doing that. But first, the little one: it would be nice to toss him about from one claw to another and then pluck off his limbs one by one.

The two were now almost paralysed with fear.

Villagers managed to pull them through the passage door just in time and slam it shut. It was a heavy wooden door, very thick, reinforced with iron strips and hinges, and for a few minutes it withstood the creature's battering.

Then the creature's hideous snout burst through the door.

Keiron looked wildly around for something to hit it with. He seized a burning branch from one of the fires which had been lit to keep the wounded warm, and ran back to the door. With sudden rage, he pressed the burning branch against the creature's nostrils. There was a scream of pain and the snout withdrew.

"Yes!" Keiron shouted, jumping up and down.

Pressing their advantage, they shoved burning wood through the broken door, and the creature backed off, hissing loudly.

With flaming branches, they drove it back up the stairs, Keiron flourishing a burning stick with the rest of them and feeling exhilarated to be doing something at last to help in the fight for his home.

Suddenly, at the top of the stairs, the dragon-like creature panicked. It blundered back into one of the rooms, smashed through the window, and was gone.

An eerie silence descended.

Keiron sank down among the debris, suddenly weak. His father sat beside him and put a shaking hand on his son's head. "You did well, my boy, very well. But we cannot stay here. At any moment another creature might come crashing through that window. We'll block the way with furniture all down the stairs."

A fat, furry insect buzzed Tara on the battlefield. Dodging this way and that, she picked up a stone and hurled it at the insect, clipping the creature's wings. The insect whirled drunkenly down at her feet, making a strangled whistling sound. Tara snarled at it in panic and it rolled away. She noticed with a shudder a row of what looked like stings sticking from its rear.

And then she was sliding and slipping on something slimy. At her feet was a sort of worm that could change its shape. It was spreading out beneath her, like a pool of obnoxious liquid, gripping her feet. She howled and fell over. It clung to her, numbing her. Several wolf-people seized her and pulled her up and away from the thing. In a few seconds, the worm returned to its original shape and it slithered away. The wolf-people let it go, not knowing how to attack so strange a life-form.

That shook her, but she fought on, joining a pack of young wolf-people whom she used to play with. They were snapping at some marine-like creature, when one of them was seized by its tentacles. He was tossed aside, apparently dead, but Tara detected life in him still. "Help me take him in to Cassie," she demanded.

It was tempting to stay inside the Mansion with him. But if she could rescue one wounded wolf-person, she could rescue others. Ignoring Cassie's pleas to stay, she steeled herself to go back out again.

In the few minutes she had been absent, things had changed on the battlefield. Many of the monsters had paused in their fighting and were listening to something strange and distant.

Faintly, with her acute hearing, Tara heard the thud-thud-thud of some heavy creature approaching the battlefield. What could it be? What new monster was Prince Badrur about to inflict on them? And why had the other creatures paused in their fighting?

As the wolf-people picked up the sound, too, a strange lull fell on the battlefield. It was not so much the sound itself which made them pause, it was its peculiar *chilling* quality.

"Like the footsteps of death," Tara said to herself with a shuddering premonition. "Coming nearer and nearer." As each footstep sounded, she felt the ground tremble beneath her paws.

CHAPTER 15

Thud-thud-thud: heavy, erratic footsteps; the Great
Salamander turned its head to listen to the sound.

The prince, whose hearing was not acute enough to
hear it yet, was alarmed at the sudden faltering in the
battle. It was time to rally his forces. With a shout of
pent-up triumph, he urged his mount forward. The
salamander half-slithered to the foot of the slope and
lumbered towards the battlefield, swaying from side to
side, trampling on everything in its path.

As soon as Lord Tancred saw Badrur make his move,
he knew it was time for him to appear on the battlefield too.

Keiron joined Cassie with the wounded. They
watched their father through a window as he edged
forward on a horse into the battle, surrounded by
villagers. Tara, still among her wolf-people, thought,
Don't let him be killed. It would break Cassie's heart.

"The greatest of his monsters is advancing upon us, "
Tancred cried. "Kill it, and the heart will go out of this
battle."

The battle picked up again, with a new ferocity.

The Great Salamander pounded forward and fell upon a group of wolf-people, scattering them with savage swipes of its tail and claws. Smelling blood, it waded in on its hind legs, scooping up anyone in its path and hurling them aside. Stones and arrows made no impression on it: only Prince Badrur was in danger from them. He clung grimly to the creature's scaly skin, hiding behind its spiky ruff.

Until then the battle had been in the balance. But the Great Salamander's bloody progress made many so weak with fear, they began to desert the battlefield, and the scales tipped. The monsters took heart from the presence of their leader and its prince and rejoined the fighting with renewed relish.

Thud-thud-thud: the mysterious sound was getting louder but few could hear it now above the noise of battle.

Lord Tancred was shaking with rage. All that he most treasured, all that linked him with his ancestors and the history of this place, was being brutally trampled on by mindless beasts and their malevolent master. He could not stand by and just exhort his forces; he would have to fight.

The twins watched him advance; their hearts were in their mouths; they knew that he was riding out of bravado, perhaps into death.

"No!" Cassie screamed. She rushed past all the wounded lying about in the corridor, out into the courtyard, Keiron close behind her. She knew there was nothing she could do, but she had to be near her father.

The twins stood in the gateway, the smell of blood,

the cries, the clashes, the wounds, the grim and mortal tangles all about them.

Keiron held on to Cassie, fearful that she would hurl herself into the battle to be with their father. They both watched terrified as he slashed the air, slicing a long, winged creature in two above his head.

In the occasional lulls in the battle sounds, the thud-thud-thud could now be heard by everyone. "Listen," said Cassie suddenly, turning to stare at the distant trees to the right of the battlefield.

"Whatever is it?" Keiron said.

But at that moment the Great Salamander spat out the body of a wolf and bellowed loudly. The sound was so bloodcurdling, everyone paused. It bellowed again, more loudly and triumphantly this time, as if trumpeting invincibility. It stimulated cries, shrieks, whirrs, thumping, screams and bellows amongst all the other hideous monsters, and the cacophony was so terrifying it broke the last shredded nerves of the villagers and wolf-people.

There was a stampede. Most of Lord Tancred's forces fled with terror in their eyes and the hideous, rampant cries of the monsters in their ears; they had had enough. Within minutes, the space between the prince and Lord Tancred was clear of villagers and wolf-people. Only a small crowd stayed around him, but he was suddenly vulnerable.

Cassie broke away from Keiron and ran forward, shouting, "Come back, Father. Come back. He'll kill you."

Tara saw her and ran towards her. She would be by Cassie's side, come what may.

"Surround her. Protect her," Keiron shouted. A few did, but others stood and watched what was unfolding before them as if they had lost the will to move. They all sensed defeat. Keiron tried to follow his sister but he was prevented: two old, wizened hands curled round his shoulders and held him. "Stay here," said Magda. "She is on her own now." Keiron turned to protest but saw such a look in her eyes, a look he could not fathom, he stayed where he was, and watched like all the others.

The prince was within hailing distance of Lord Tancred.

"Surrender now," Badrur shouted.

Tancred made a contemptuous gesture with his sword.

"You will be torn to shreds," Badrur warned.

"Come away, Father," shouted Cassie in a torment.

But Lord Tancred was fired up and beyond reason. He spurred his horse forward. It neighed and reared, terrified. He spurred it harder, savagely digging his heels into its sides.

The Great Salamander slithered forward, baring its teeth.

The horse neighed wildly, reared – and then, in extreme fear, it suddenly buckled and crumpled beneath its rider. Tancred narrowly missed being crushed by the collapsing horse. As he staggered to his feet, villagers and wolf-people, the few that were left, surrounded him. They waited fatefully for the salamander to take its first pick of them.

The horse twitched and then fell silent.

In the relative quiet that ensued, everyone could hear a crashing sound in the trees.

Puzzled, Prince Badrur ordered his mount to rise on its hind legs so that he might see what was approaching.

The creature, salivating, was not pleased to be interrupted at such a moment, and Badrur had to swivel his body around the ruff and look into its eye to hypnotize it again. The creature rose to its greatest height.

Everyone turned.

Badrur saw her first. The Child. She had grown enormously since he had last seen her and she was now almost as tall as a man. And yet, judging by the heavy thud of her bare footsteps, she must weigh far more than any human. Covered in a sort of tunic that she had made for herself out of animals' skins, her arms and face streaked with mud, she blundered from the trees into the scrubland, attracted by the noise of the battle. She paused in delight when she saw the prince. He was the one she had been looking for ever since she had looked into his eyes. She thudded forward, waving her great pudgy arms about excitedly.

Everyone looked at her with amazement. Somehow, she seemed more outlandish than any other creature the villagers and wolf-people had fought that day. And as she stumbled closer, they saw how deadened her eyes were, deep pools with no expression.

"It's as if she's blind," Cassie murmured, shuddering.

"She can see," Tara objected.

"Only with her eyes. Not with her heart. She's a dead thing inside, remember? And I'm the one who brought her back to this earth."

She's so huge, Keiron said.

She feeds off death, that's why, said Will. *Like the vine that sucks the life from a tree.*

The Child swiped at a puffball insect hovering near her head, knocking it to the ground. Annoyed, she stooped and touched it and its twitching stopped. As she straightened up, she appeared fractionally bigger. Or was that just an illusion?

The Child began to run on her stubby legs towards Prince Badrur, burbling delightedly.

"Kill her!" he shouted to the monsters around him.

They surged towards the Child.

She stopped, a deep scowl on her face.

As the creatures hurled themselves at her, and bombed her and tried to sting or bite her, they felt her touch of death freeze their blood and hearts. They fell away from her, until their corpses were like a rampart around her. She was laughing now, enjoying herself, and she had grown bigger too: this was no illusion. Every death was life to her; every touch of it gave her new strength: that was why she was so big and growing bigger all the time.

Then there was nothing but dead bodies between the Child and Badrur. She ambled towards him, a peculiar look of longing on her face. The Great Salamander shied away in terror.

Despair struck at Prince Badrur's heart. Victory had been in his grasp, and then... He looked into the dark emptiness of the Child's eyes and shuddered.

"Rise up," he barked at what were left of his monsters, "and take us out of here."

He threw one furious glance at Tancred, as if to say, "You've won this time, but I'll be back," and wheeled his monster round in fast retreat.

The remnants of his frightened horde of creatures flew off, lumbered, crashed, slithered and scampered away from the battlefield as fast as they could, with shrieks and bellows. Among them was Aulic, more terrified than he had ever been in his life. The Child lumbered after them, waving her arms about and shrieking with pleasure.

Those that were left – Lord Tancred and his children, Tara, Magda and a few faithful villagers and wolf-people – watched their departure with a trembling relief.

"Let us get away from this place of death," Tancred said to his children, thankful to find them unscathed, still shaking from his ordeal.

But they had barely reached the gates when someone cried, "The Child is coming back!" The Child, realizing she could not catch up with Badrur, had turned back, frustrated and puzzled.

She caught sight of Cassie: there was something familiar about that girl...

Cassie stumbled forward, her arms outstretched, her face ghostlike; she was pulled forward by a force she did not understand. As the Child advanced towards her, the girl seemed to drown in her devouring eyes. She slowed to a halt and stood there, fatalistically.

Tara, still in her wolf-skin, darted back to Cassie and tried vainly to head her off.

The Child, now bigger than any man, having fed off the death of so many monsters, loomed over the two of them. She reached down towards Cassie, murmuring softly to herself.

Defiantly, Tara leapt between Cassie and the Child. She was trembling all over now, but her eyes were blazing with all the cunning and courage of her wolfish blood and with all the love of her human heart. She knew she was doomed, but if it gave them time to save Cassie. . .

The Child reached out to brush the wolf-girl aside. Tara dodged this, and the Child tried again. Leaping this way and that, Tara distracted the Child and drew her away from Cassie, enough for the others to creep forward, ready to grab the girl. But seeing this, the Child made a lunge for them; she stumbled and, losing her balance, she fell over. Her weight made the ground shake. She sat up, angry.

And then, with an unexpected swipe she seized hold of Cassie by the hair and dragged her towards her. She did not mean to be rough, it was just her way, but Cassie screamed in pain, terrified. Surprised, the Child let go of her.

Tara instinctively raced towards the Child, her teeth bared. The Child swiped her aside. Tara flung herself at the Child again, aware that the distraction she was causing allowed Cassie to crawl away. The wolf-girl saw Keiron and Tancred grab hold of the girl – and that was her last conscious moment.

The Child seized Tara by the scruff of her neck and wrenched her up into the air. She shook the wolf-girl angrily from side to side and squeezed her. For a second, Tara's eyes flared with agony. Then the life went out of her and her body went limp.

She died instantly.

Cassie saw the terrible sacrifice. She screamed Tara's name over and over uncontrollably. Magda held her in her arms and tried to shield her, but Cassie insisted on seeing what was happening.

The Child swung the wolf-girl's body around as if it was

a doll. Then she clambered to her feet and dropped Tara's limp, broken form on to the blood-soaked mud, among the rest of the bodies. Her eyes were now on Cassie. Why were they taking the girl away from her?

"Into the Mansion. Quick," said Tancred.

They dragged the screaming girl towards the Mansion gates and just managed to close them in time against the lumbering Child.

For a while, she banged on the doors with her great fists. Then she roamed around the deserted battlefield, grizzling.

They watched from the Mansion windows as she set off in the direction which Prince Badrur had taken. She stumbled up the ridge and stood for a moment, swaying darkly on the horizon.

Cassie rushed out to reclaim Tara's body. She sobbed over the broken wolf-girl. She was inconsolable.

CHAPTER 16

Keiron and his father wandered among the wounded downstairs, giving comfort where they could. Keiron felt desperately sorry for the pain they were in, and at times his stomach turned at the sight of a wound, a lost leg, a missing eye. As he steeled himself to look at the corpses being carried out to be buried, as he thought of Tara's sacrifice to save his sister, a darkness crept into his veins, a hatred for all things monstrous and evil. Shaken, he returned to his father's side.

"You should take the children to your ship," said Magda to Tancred as she hurried by with some salve for a wound.

Cassie came in, her eyes dark, her face streaked with tears. "We must bury her before we go," she said hoarsely.

"Of course," said Magda, folding her in her arms. "But there is plenty of time for that. It will be done properly, with all her pack around her."

Cassie pressed herself against the old woman. Then she disengaged herself, wiped her eyes and said, "I have some healing to do."

They watched her in admiration as she began to move among the wounded.

With so many wounded still in the Mansion, they decided to stay there too for a little while longer, despite the wreckage upstairs.

Cassie, exhausted and full of the most aching grief, did as much as she could in the sick-rooms until Magda insisted on her going to bed. The medicine woman gave her a sleeping draught.

When Keiron looked in on her, she seemed barely to breathe. He watched her for a long time, fearful of the effect Tara's death might have on her.

Then he felt some invisible stirring in the room – just the air, perhaps, but he looked around, thinking of Tara. How empty the room seemed without her. He longed for her to appear, longed for her slanted grey eyes and her quick, flicking movements. He felt something brush his hair, like a coil of breath, but there was nothing there. Sadness crept over him. He sat on the rug where Tara invariably slept at the foot of Cassie's bed, and closed his eyes. But his head was full of battle scenes, of blood, of slashing claws that would not let him rest. He rose, looked again at his sister sleeping peacefully, and stole out.

He found his father staring sadly at the chaos and destruction in his study.

"It's no use," said Lord Tancred. "All my work is in tatters. I can never rebuild this."

"You could try," Keiron offered, sensing a note of resignation in father's voice which alarmed him.

"No, not here. Prince Badrur will attack again, there is

no doubt of that, and I fear he will succeed eventually. We shall be forced to flee. It's only a matter of time. And besides, how can I put together half a lifetime's work again? All my books destroyed, my maps and globes and charts. Everything! A line has been drawn in the sand here, and I cannot cross it." He sighed, covered his eyes with his hand and bent his head.

"We won the battle," Keiron said, trying to comfort him.

"But not, I fear, the war."

Keiron wondered what to do. It was still light, and after such a day the thought of calmly going to bed, as if everything was normal, seemed impossible to him.

Something was in the back of his mind. . .

The Helmet!

What about it? said Will suspiciously. He had been measuring the progress of the battle by the images in Keiron's head and by the pace of the boy's heartbeat. He now judged it safe to re-emerge from the tight ball he'd made of himself in Keiron's breast pocket. Battles were stupid affairs. No one ever gained anything from them.

Where is it?

Haven't you had enough of that wretched thing? It nearly froze you to death, remember?

For some time a ghost of an idea had been gathering in Keiron's mind. Now it flashed across his imagination. Voices! A thousand voices! That was the way to defeat Badrur and the monsters.

What now?

Do you know where the Helmet is? I must find it.

Why do you need to ask me?

Taking the hint, Keiron questioned the broken chairs, the split wainscot, the shattered vases, the torn rugs, as to the whereabouts of the Helmet. Of course, all they wanted to talk about was the damage done to themselves and who was going to put it right. Keiron had to make a lot of false promises about that before they would divulge what they knew of its whereabouts. Eventually he found the Golden Helmet under a heap of shredded tapestry outside his father's study.

He carried it to his own room and sat on the bed.

How bright, how unblemished the Helmet looked, its gold softly glinting. And yet the dark slits in its visor were like black, unfathomable eyes, and he kept staring at the Helmet, turning it in his hands, fascinated by its terrible power. This was what had roused the monsters from centuries of slumber. Should he do it? Should he put it on his head and use its power to magnify his gift?

How will you use it? asked Will alarmed. Didn't these humans ever learn?

I'll send out a message.

Ah! said Will, beginning to understand. *And that message would be?*

Get out of here! Keiron answered fiercely.

For a second, Will was startled. Had he offended his friend? Then he understood. *Oh, you mean...?* Will chuckled.

Well, it might work. Keiron knew he hadn't much time; darkness would fall soon, and Cassie had told him that if you put the Helmet on at night, you woke things of the night.

Yes, it might work, Will echoed. *But even if it doesn't, it won't do any lasting harm, and it might just give those monsters a few sleepless nights. Try it!*

Gleefully, but apprehensively, Keiron raised the Golden Helmet. Should he do it? His hands trembled.

Go on, Will urged impatiently.

I'm scared.

Look, you ought to have at least one go of it. And it's still light. Use your gift. Go on.

So Keiron slowly lowered the Helmet over his head for the first – and last – time.

Will was sitting on his knee and Keiron could see the little manikin through the visor.

Well, how does it feel?

A bit dark. Echoey. Warm, too.

Concentrate, then. Think of your message, then think of each thing in turn and send the message to it. I think that'll channel your power.

Right.

Keiron took a deep breath. First, he pictured the stone walls of the Ice Castle. Through the extraordinary magnifying power of the goddess's Helmet he transmitted the following message to the stones. *When the monsters return, tell them every minute of the day and the night to go, to get out, to leave this island for good. Just keep dinning that into their thick skulls, all right? And never stop until you drive them out of their minds and they leave. Keep chanting go, go, go and leave, leave, leave into their heads until it drives them mad.*

He pictured rocks, trees, bushes, stones, tracks, huts, weapons, utensils, everything he could imagine that the monsters might come in contact with, and he gave them the same message. He felt the power of the Helmet ripple across the land like a fast-moving and spreading wind, delivering his message. Each time he transmitted it, he grew more elated: he sensed that the things liked his message and that they would do his bidding. The whole island would turn against them; everything they came in contact with would demand that they leave. What a brilliant idea!

He sensed that he had used up what power he had; his mind went dark. He eased off the Helmet and grinned at Will. *That should get rid of the monsters. And without them, Badrur is nothing.*

"I wonder what Cassie will think of what I've done," he said to himself a little later. He couldn't keep this news to himself; he went to see if she was awake.

He placed the Helmet at the foot of the bed where Tara used to sleep.

Cassie was still breathing softly but she looked very cold. There was blue around her eyes and a pallor in her skin. When he took her hand its was limp and icy. He was worried. Should he tell Magda?

Just warm her up yourself, Will suggested.

He got into bed beside her and tried to warm her with his body. She stirred and murmured in her sleep. He felt her sadness, even in sleep, at Tara's death. *Poor Cass. I'll be here to look after you.*

And then, suddenly very tired, he fell asleep too.

Lord Tancred paced the ruins of the Mansion. He was sickened by what he saw. There were many parts of the building they could move into while repairs were being done, but he had an overwhelming desire now to cut loose, to set sail – to get away from North Island. For his children's sake, too – he could not allow them to fall into Badrur's traitorous hands. His life here had been poisoned.

He opened his study window and looked at the sea glinting in the evening light. The crow's nest of his ship was just visible and he kept his eye on it as he dreamed of their escape to a new life.

CHAPTER 17

In the stampede from the battlefield, Aulic had been separated from the other men and he was making his way back to the Ice Castle on his own. It was a hazardous journey. He skirted villages, he kept a sharp look out for wolf-people, he slept in ditches, hollows, trappers' huts, even one night in the crook of a tree. He grew ravenous and resorted to chewing muddy roots. He was drenched by sheets of hissing rain, battered by hail, made miserable by seemingly never-ending sleet, and the wind delighted in pushing him about and freezing his aching bones. What a cursed place this island is, he said to himself.

From time to time he felt the earth vibrate with the Child's heavy tread and it filled him with terror. Why was she taking the same route to the Ice Castle? Or was she dogging him?

As he made his way north, the air grew colder, more biting. The earth hardened, the wind pinched his hands, feet and face with freezing pincers, and frost glittered on his clothes when he woke at dawn.

But it wasn't the weather that really troubled him. It was the curious signs of something else. There was a strange panic in the air.

He noticed it first when he saw flying monsters weave about drunkenly in the air above the trees. One spiralled down and crouched not far from the tree where he had taken shelter. It was shaking its scaly head from side to side as if it had a sting in its ear. Driven to distraction, it shook its wings and managed to get airborne again. Aulic watched puzzled as it crashed up through the leaves. He noticed that it no longer flew in the direction of the Ice Castle.

Then he was startled by a huge centipede-like creature hurrying across his path, emitting a high-pitched whine. He watched its erratic course, noticing how it seemed to swerve away from trees and rocks and any large objects like logs when normally these would not have disturbed it. How strange. It, too, was heading away from the Ice Castle.

As he trudged his way cautiously towards the Castle, he saw more and more signs among the monsters of panicky flight. They all seemed to be heading in the same direction – he supposed towards the coast. Some just stood bemused and paralysed, their eyes stricken, but most gave the impression of being prodded, goaded, hounded forward against their will, all shaking their heads as if to get rid of... What? It was as if they were being tormented in their heads. Was this Badrur's doing? And yet, how could it be? Surely the prince would be marshalling his forces for another assault on the Mansion?

Filthy, perished, starving and exhausted, he finally reached the castle.

He walked wearily into the courtyard. It was eerily quiet.

There was no sign of Prince Badrur, no monsters. Inside the castle, there were only cold ashes in the grates. In mounting despair, Aulic wandered through the freezing, gloomy castle, calling out feebly.

Eventually, he heard faint cries in answer to his calls. He found several of Badrur's men, all wounded from the battle, holed up in a dormitory, abandoned by their master. At first they welcomed him, thinking that he heralded the return of Badrur, but when he told them his story, they grew surly and silent.

"But where is he?" he asked, baffled by the men's depression. "Why has he gone?"

"The stones spoke," said one man. "The trees, the rocks outside, the walls, the windows, the bowls and plates inside, everything spoke against the monsters."

Aulic was mystified.

"That was what Badrur told us," said another. "The Great Salamander said the Island was telling them to leave, was chanting it in their heads and driving them crazy. They had no choice."

Now he understood the strange behaviour of the creatures.

"Where have they gone?"

"To the coast. They're leaving the island."

"And Prince Badrur has gone with them?" Aulic asked with a groan, his spirits plummeting further.

"He had no choice. Without them, he is nothing."

Several of the men spat on the floor in a collective show of disgust at the mention of their master.

"So he left you to your wounds."

"As you see."

"What about Angharer?"

"She went with him, of course. You don't think she'd stay behind to look after the likes of us, do you?"

He was aware that all the men were watching him.

"*You* could look after us until we get better," one of them said.

In that appeal he sensed an ill-defined threat. He stared back at them. He knew he could leave now, leave them perhaps to die of their wounds. Or he could stay and tend them as best as he could.

In the end, it wasn't fear or conscience that helped him decide, it was weariness. He'd had enough of running. He would stay. Looking after them would give him something to do and it might just earn their gratitude.

They were woken in the night by a loud, rhythmic, rumbling noise. Peering down into the moonlit courtyard, they saw a dark shadow. "It's that monstrous Child," one of the men whispered. What they could hear was the Child breathing heavily, almost snoring, in her sleep.

In the morning, hungry and frustrated, she banged on the walls and doors of the Castle, trying to break in. She demolished a wooden shed with gigantic kicks and threw the splintered wood about the courtyard.

All morning she sat among the debris, snivelling and crooning, hoping Badrur would appear; but by midday, hunger drove her out. There was little for her to eat in this part of the island, and she was reduced to pulling up bushes and chewing their rubbery leaves to ease her hunger pains. Fortified, she stumbled on, following the signs – the broken branches, the trampled bushes, the churned mud – that told her that this was the way the monsters had gone. Where they were, so would Badrur be.

She pushed on and on, her energy seemingly inexhaustible, pounding the earth with her heavy, encrusted feet; until a few days later she came to the harbour.

It was deserted. All the boats and ships had gone.

In the water were the bodies of many of the monsters, drowned days before in their panic to leave – the chant in their heads to go, go, go, leave, leave, leave, having driven them mad. Their bodies were now monstrously swollen, tossing on the rough waves, piling on the beach in obscene and putrefying mounds.

Even the Child was affected by the smell. She held her nose and shook her head.

Further up the coast she settled down and sat for days by the sea.

A few late flying monsters passed overhead.

She was half aware of being watched from a distance by the harbour people. They had fled as soon as Prince Badrur and his army of monsters had appeared and set sail. Now they were creeping back. Their houses had been smashed, their gardens trampled into the mud. The Child picked her way through the ruins, playing with the furniture, eating what she could; but she was going through the motions now, it wasn't fun any more. Nothing was.

One day she waded far out into the choppy waters. The undercurrents swept her off her feet. It scared her a bit, but she liked the sensation of being carried by the sea, bobbing along on its waves. Then she saw a ship pass in the distance and she knew what she had to do.

She began to swim. It was an awkward, doggy, splashy swim, but she was able to move forward, out to sea. Soon she got into a rhythm and made progress. The ship appeared on the horizon again and she followed it.

In Lord Tancred's dreams, a mysterious silver cat kept appearing. He felt close to her, although she always stayed just out of reach of his hand. She was like a spirit, he thought. He took to going to the Chapel at odd hours of the day, and sitting in its silence as if waiting for a message. One day he came out of the Chapel with a new look in his eye. He said to his children, "I now believe that we must return the Helmet to Temple Island. It should be reunited with the Golden Armour that remains there."

Cassie remembered the voice she had heard in the wind while she was in the crow's nest, and she nodded.

"Has it done its job, then?" Keiron wondered. If so, with the weather having reverted so quickly to its normal harshness, it wasn't very effective.

He and his father looked at Cassie.

She shook her head – not just to answer Keiron's question, but because the Helmet had become so hateful to her. In her mind she linked it with the death of Tara.

But always there was a presence in her room, the presence of Tara, unseen but uncannily felt, which took the edge away from her unhappiness. And Tara kept whispering to her. *Put on the Helmet one last time and finish its work.*

She daren't. What if it was a false voice telling her to do that? Or her own imagination? Hadn't she done enough damage?

She was sitting alone one morning in the great hall, drawing pictures in the dust on the table, when Keiron appeared. He was carrying the Helmet. She shrank back from it. "If I hadn't put it on that second time. . ." she cried, banging her fists on the table in anger at herself.

"Stop it, Cassie," Keiron shouted.

"What did you bring it to me for?" she shouted back.

"Will told me to."

"Huh!" she exclaimed; but the answer was so oddly funny, the anger went out of her and she shrugged. "Oh, I might have known it. Wooden Brain!"

Will, who was sitting in Keiron's hair, said, *She hasn't finished with it yet. Tell her.*

He told her.

She scowled at the Helmet. "I don't want to," she said, turning away.

There was an awkward silence.

"Well, what does he say to that?" she asked, exasperated.

Will said, *Shouldn't Tara be buried in a paradise? Doesn't she deserve that?*

Keiron repeated this.

Cassie stiffened. They had buried Tara on a grassy knoll deep within the woods where she had been born. It had been a solemn occasion, led by Magda and largely conducted by the wolf-people. She had been buried in her human form, for they knew that was what she would have wanted; and they gave her skin to Cassie, who hugged it to herself and cried over it. The rain had beaten down on them, dashing away her tears... Yes, Will was right, Tara deserved more than cold rain seeping about her.

"What if it all goes wrong again?" she whispered.

"It's not night," said Keiron. "You'll turn the things of day, of light and all that, into – well, a paradise. That's what Will reckons. And he usually knows what he's on about."

"Does he?" she muttered sceptically; but she took the Helmet that Keiron slid across the table to her.

In the firelight it had a fantastic glitter. Smears of dirt and ash, tiny scratches and dents, told of its rough fortunes. That made it seem to her less awe-inspiring, less formidable.

She would do it for Tara's sake.

Keiron lowered the Helmet over her head.

She closed her eyes and thought intensely, longingly of sunshine. She thought of sunshine on brick, of sunlight glancing off bright leaves and penetrating into buds and bulbs. She thought of sunlight on fur and wing, glittering on water, melting snow and ice. She thought of warmth making its way into the wolves' lairs and into Magda's cave. She thought of leaves unfurling and young animals staggering into first light. She thought of the wind sweeping away the clouds and dying to a whisper; she saw the sky turn blue.

In the brilliance of the Helmet, she felt the earth begin to thaw deep within its many layers.

Then she thought of the sunlight on Tara's grave, on the mound of moss and the flowers there – and she knew that, however long she kept her transforming thoughts on that, she would never be able to bring the wolf-girl back to life. She had learnt that bitter lesson. But at least Tara could rest in a place that would always be beautiful.

She somehow knew that this was the last time she would consent to use the Golden Helmet, and her life-giving force had to be be stretched to the limit. She concentrated hard, she went into a kind of trance, she lost track of time.

North Island was healing. The Helmet magnified her life-force and the island began to purge itself of centuries of coldness, of darkness, of death.

At last, birds filled the silence with uncertain song. Cassie heard them, clear and sublime, in her head, and it seemed like a signal to her that her work was done.

The Helmet came off easily. Its gold light shone in her eyes.

Keiron could feel warm currents about his feet. He could hear that the world outside was no longer moaning with wind or being lashed with rain. "You've done it," he shouted. "Come on, let's go out and see."

They ran outside. The corpses of dead monsters still

lay about, but they ignored them. The sky was dazzling blue, the warmth of the sunlight on their faces was wonderful, and the peaceful silence made them want to shout out their glee. Lord Tancred came out of the Chapel and held out his hands in disbelief; then, giving Cassie a searching look, he guessed what had happened. Some villagers, who had come as servants to the Mansion, ran out too, jabbering excitedly.

When they had calmed down, Tancred said, "I feel this will last. There's a rightness about it. It's like a world waking up after a long sleep."

"Let's go out and see what's happened in the island," said Keiron.

"Oh, yes, let's," said Cassie, taking her father's arm.

"When we're quite sure it's safe to do so," said Tancred.

Reports had come to him from the northern part of the island of the exodus of the monsters from the castle, Badrur among them. Their progress towards the coast was being tracked; but he did not yet know that they had fled. He had heard, too, of the strange, tormented behaviour of the creatures. When told of this, Keiron confessed what he had done and he had become something of a hero. Full hero status was still in doubt, however, for the monster army could swerve back towards the Mansion at any time if the din in their heads didn't last.

Now the sunshine on their skin, in their hair and eyes, and on their bare arms, seemed to be saying the battle was over. The island was at peace again; nature was finding its balance; the land was healing.

* * *

199

As the island burst back into life, Tancred and the twins spent weeks exploring inland. The rains were gentle now, the heat comfortable, the quiet wind cooling. Plants flourished everywhere, insects hatched and scampered about their business happily, birds built nests and trilled, and the animals revelled in their new world, sniffing everything fresh in their path.

They came at last to the harbour where Badrur had set sail and where the Child had lingered before following him. The harbour people were busy rebuilding their houses.

The life briefly drained out of Cassie when she heard about the Child.

Looking out over the calm sea, Keiron put his arm around his sister and said, "She'll drown out there, Cass. She can't swim for ever."

"She might come back."

"She might. But Badrur's not here. That's who she wants, not us. And if she does survive, let's hope she'll follow Badrur to the ends of the earth."

"I wish..." she whispered vehemently. But the wish died in her throat.

Lord Tancred brought the children into the Chapel. The Helmet was on the altar. It had been cleaned and was gleaming now in the soft sunlight slanting through the windows.

"What have we come here for, then?" Cassie asked.

"It was here that I was told... Well, I think we should go on a voyage."

"A voyage?" the twins echoed, startled.

"Yes, to Temple Island. You remember I told you we have to return the Golden Helmet."

"Oh, great!" Keiron exclaimed, delighted. Travel at last!

"Temple Island," Cassie murmured. The fabled place of legend, tiny, deserted, always beautiful, with the ruined temple at its centre. Yes, she thought, that's the one place in all the world I'd rather be now.

A week later, they boarded the ship to begin their journey. The crew raised some of the sails and took their trunks down to their cabins.

The Mansion was left in the care of village helpers. Tancred tried to persuade Magda to move into the house in their absence, to keep an eye on things, but she preferred her cave. "It's like a little paradise all in itself, now things are quiet and warm," she said. "But I'll make sure your precious Mansion remains safe, and the damage is repaired."

She was at the quayside, among the villagers and trappers, when they were about to leave, surrounded by wolf-people.

The twins climbed the crow's nest. They waved to the crowd on the quay, and to Magda in particular.

"Look at the island now," said Cassie. "Isn't it beautiful."

It blazed with colour and a hundred shades of green.

"Funny we should be leaving it just when we've got what we've wished for," said Keiron, a sudden lump in his throat.

"We'll be back," said Cassie. With Tara's death still like a shadow in her heart, she had fewer regrets.

They sat close together and let the wind comb out their straggly hair.

Some of the waiting crowd below began to call for the Helmet. They had heard of its discovery but had never seen it.

The twins shinned down the rope ladder and stood by their father's side as he held up the Golden Helmet for all to see. Great flashes of light glanced off it, and the few cheers that emerged from the crowd at sight of it were swallowed up in an awed silence. They all knew that they owed the miraculous transformation of their island to this mesmerizing object.

Tancred turned and held the Helmet directly up to the sun. He felt a powerful tingling, a current of light, pass through him.

And then the most amazing thing happened, something entirely unexpected.

A tunnel of light began to form. It was just a streak of yellow mist at first, but it formed rapidly into something like a golden rainbow that curved up from the Helmet and over the brilliant sea. It was so big, they found themselves looking down a golden highway made of light.

The light swirled around them and enveloped the whole ship.

They stood together, unable to speak, their eyes, hair, clothes, glittering in the light all around them.

Then the ship moved. It shifted slowly, effortlessly, so that its stern faced into the tunnel of light. The twins clung to their father. By slow degrees, the ship lifted itself out of the water. It turned majestically and floated into the tunnel entrance.

Magda, and all those on the quay, watched in amazement as the ship slowly disappeared down the golden highway, its sails now full, its progress serene and silent.

CHAPTER 18

The ship floated steadily and silently down the tunnel of light. Decks, ropes and sails, polished wood and brass, were gilded with gold. They stood on the bridge, bathed in the warm light.

Will sat in Keiron's hair, his green eyes closed; he had visions of a great, whispering willow tree, brilliant with new leaves.

Cassie whispered to herself, "Tara, I wish you were coming with us."

They drifted silently through the light. It had a healing effect, so that in time their aches and sadness, and the terrible images of the battle that flashed across their minds, were soothed away.

Time seemed suspended.

"Citatha is guarding us against treacherous waters," Lord Tancred observed. "Many ships have gone down in that sea."

Cassie took her father's arm. "Do you think we shall see Citatha when we get to Temple Island?"

"See her?" Tancred chuckled. "I don't think anyone has *seen* her. But it is quite possible that she will speak to us."

"I wonder what she will say," said Keiron.

His father shrugged. "To thank us, perhaps, for finding the Helmet and bringing it back to her."

"For healing North Island," Cassie added, dreamily, thinking of the wonderful transformation of her home.

Tancred smiled. "We were caught up in currents of magic, good and bad," he said. "On Temple Island, things will be different."

Will murmured, *Oh, has he forgotten that Temple Island is the most magical place of all?*

Yes, but we shall come to no harm there.

Hmm, Will answered sceptically. *Perhaps not there.*

Keiron sighed. *Out with it. Come on. What do you see ahead?*

My sap drying up! Too much sunlight, not enough water.

Is that all?

It'll be enough, said Will grimly. The manikin, once more catching a glimpse of the future, saw deserts, with little plant life except grass and cacti in a waste of sand, and it was a sort of hell to him.

After what seemed many days, the tunnel of light began to slope gently downwards. Presently they saw far ahead the coast of Temple Island. In their excitement, they said nothing, gripping the rail of the bridge, biting back their impatience at the ship's measured pace. The circle at the tunnel's end grew wider and wider and filled with a landscape of sand, soft lapping sea, palm trees and bushes with crimson and blue flowers.

Slowly, the ship lowered itself. They heard the splash and flow of water and felt the ship rock. The tunnel of light dissolved and they were exposed, suddenly, to a perfect blue sky filled with curious, swooping birds. The ship manoeuvred into a natural harbour and the anchor was dropped.

Lord Tancred rowed the twins across the clear water to the shore. The Golden Helmet, nestling in a wooden casket, was by his side.

He stood on the sand and looked about him, thinking how beautiful the place was. Keiron pulled in the boat.

Cassie took in deep breaths of pure air. It was good to be on solid ground again.

As they progressed inland, several feral cats, lean and sleek in their silvered fur, flitted through the foliage ahead of them. Grapes hung from vines, citrus fruit shone among the leaves, huge blooms with heavy scents littered their path, beautiful grasses and shrubs stirred in the warm breeze, and small mammals scampered out of their way or watched from trees as they passed.

"This island is casting its spell on me," Cassie said dreamily, running her hands through a clump of fine, silky grass that reached to her shoulders.

"I'm not surprised," said Tancred. "You know what this is a fragment of?"

"What do you mean?" Keiron asked.

"This is a fragment of that huge paradisal island the goddess once ruled over before the Great Volcano split it into five. The climate stayed the same here, under her protection. You can see why she wants all the islands to be like it, can't you. North Island will be as beautiful, as enchanting, as this place, you'll see."

Will was in ecstasy. *This is the sort of place where*

trees go when they die, he said. *Where nature rules, not humans.*

Keiron smiled. *Don't get too enthusiastic. We're only passing through, remember.*

"Why are there no paths?" Cassie wondered.

"No one lives here, that's why," said Keiron.

"But why not?"

"I've read that people have tried to settle here," said their father, "but no one has stayed long. The place, they say, is haunted by the spirits of the priestesses that once tended the temple: they drive the intruders out."

Cassie shivered and looked about her apprehensively.

Before long they came upon the ruins of a once great temple. Huge tawny bricks and broken slabs, crumbling columns and shattered statues, tangles of ivy and brambles, glints of silver from the swarming cats: the effect was breathtaking and melancholy.

"It's just like the pictures you've shown us of it," Keiron pointed out.

"Yes," said Cassie. "It makes me feel that I've been here before."

"But nothing really prepares you for the reality," Tancred added.

He pointed to what was once a magnificent entrance, now strewn with broken beams and sundered blocks. It led into the ruin. They had to pick their way carefully over rubble and tough, snaking plants. Soon they came to the steps which led down into the vaults.

Here the silence was extraordinary.

They stepped over some rubble, under an arch and entered a huge, domed chamber. Light flooded down from a jagged hole in the ceiling. There were a few dried leaves on the flagstones, and some plants growing in crevices, but otherwise the chamber was curiously clean, no dust, no cobwebs, no signs of animal life.

Their eyes were drawn to a platform in the centre of the chamber. It was like an altar, carved elaborately with images of cats and lizards and plants.

And there it was, lying ghostly, like a gleaming body, in the dark.

The Golden Armour lay on an altar, incomplete. Its gloves rested on its breastplate, softly reflecting the sunlight. They had seen countless drawings and paintings of it, and had read many descriptions of it, but nothing had prepared them for the awe it inspired in them. On the surface it looked almost like an ordinary suit of armour; but the legend deep within it, the aura of the goddess around it, the strange pathos of its incompleteness, moved and thrilled them.

Yet without its helmet, it looked horribly unfinished, like a body without a head.

Tancred's hands trembled. "I shall give the Helmet back to the Armour now," he announced. He handed the casket containing the Helmet to Cassie, opened the lid, and lifted it out. It cast a beam of soft light over the Armour.

Cassie shivered, recalling its power to freeze North Island and raise the monsters from their ancient sleep; but Keiron touched it once more, remembering how it had helped him drive the monsters from their home.

Lord Tancred held the Helmet above the Armour, chanted something unintelligible to the twins, then, his hands still shaking, he lowered it into place. Although there was no sound, the Helmet seemed to connect at once with the rest of the Armour. All of it, from Helmet to golden foot, began to glow. They stepped back and felt the light intensify until the whole chamber was illuminated.

As leaves are stirred by the wind, so suddenly the light seemed stirred by a current.

The goddess Citatha was there in the chamber. They knew it at once although they could not see her. She had a strangely paradoxical effect on them – making them feel both supremely confident, as if they could achieve anything they set their minds to, and at the same time utterly insignificant, like specks of dust.

Then she spoke. "I have watched your progress," she said, "with great joy and trepidation." Her voice was like a coil of wind in a hollow chamber. "You have suffered much to bring the Helmet back to me. I shall not forget the debt I owe you."

Cassie and Keiron looked searchingly about them. They felt their scalps prickle. Lord Tancred drew them both to him and put his arms around their shoulders.

The goddess's disembodied voice filled the vault. "One of the four great islands is at last returned to its original state – you, Cassie, I chiefly thank for that. It has been purged of its ancient enemies, for which I thank you, Keiron. You have remarkable children, Lord Tancred: they are your greatest treasure."

Tancred bowed slightly; the twins were too over-awed to respond.

"Over the years, many people have made their way to this vault. Most of them reached the outer chamber before I had to bar their way. They were not the Chosen Ones. Each time I hoped... But now at last I have found you. You have proved yourselves magnificently."

They seemed to hear her sighing.

"You are hoping to go back to North Island," she continued, the tone of her voice changing. "To enjoy the transformation of your home. In time you will; but not yet. There is still much for you to do."

"What is it you wish from us?" Tancred managed to say.

"The Golden Helmet waited in the tomb for centuries. The three other parts – the Shield, the Spurs and the Sword – are waiting too."

Tancred gasped; in a flash, he saw what she intended for them. The twins glanced at each other too, wondering if they had understood her. Will, spreadeagled in Keiron's hair, sighed to himself – it was just as he thought, forget the forests of North Island; they wouldn't be going home just yet.

The goddess sensed their dismay. "East Island is dying for lack of water," she explained. "It is burning up. There is no rain, and the water in the caverns beneath the earth is receding. There is only one spring, and that is controlled by Prince Badrur's mother.

"Somewhere in that kingdom is the Golden Shield. Many have stumbled across it over the centuries and not recognized it for what it was. You are different. You must find it and release its power."

Now the twins understood. They felt the pressure of their father's hands on their shoulders, willing them to say nothing as yet.

"You must find it and use it to bring rain to the parched land. I want you to transform East Island into a paradise, just as you did with your home. Only you can do it."

There was a long pause. Was she waiting for an answer? But to Tancred it seemed like an order that he could not disobey.

"I shall go now to North Island," she said at last, her voice softening again. "You have made that possible for me, for I can only exist where nature is in harmony."

The light stirred again.

"Won't you tell us where the Shield is hidden?" asked Keiron, venturing to speak for the first time.

There was no answer.

"Please," said Cassie.

They listened to the silence.

"I fear she has gone," said Tancred. "She has thanked us, she has given us our mission..."

"But why us?" Cassie wondered. "Why have we been chosen?"

"No one can answer that," their father said.

"Well, what do we do now?" Keiron wondered.

"It's simple," Tancred sighed. "We must set sail for East Island."

For one last time, they touched the Golden Helmet, which had brought so much joy and heartache and danger into their lives, feeling its subtle vibrations of energy.

Then they left the Armour glowing in its vault, and made their way out.

They emerged from the ruins into brilliant sunlight. The silver cats mewed and milled about their feet. The children wanted to linger on the island, tasting the fruit, looking at the strange wildlife, running to stretch their limbs and enjoy the freedom, but the cats, with hypnotic insistence, urged them on, leading them towards the ship and mewing strangely at every delay.

They reached the shore and reluctantly clambered into the boat. As they rowed towards the ship, Cassie said, "Please let's stay here for a while."

But in this her father was powerless. That night as they slept, the ship mysteriously lifted anchor and floated off over the calm sea.

It headed straight towards the shores of East Island, and to another whole world of danger and excitement. Their adventures had only just begun.

Continue the search...

THE SHIELD

Each day the climate grew hotter and drier. The twins enjoyed developing a deep, walnut tan – it was a new experience for them, having been brought up in such a cold, sunless climate – but as the ship approached East island, the heat became a little too intense and uncomfortable.

The island appeared as a dark smudge at first on the flashing waters, but soon stretched out along the sky-line. Low, sandy-coloured buildings and a few trees became visible, with many small ships bobbing on the coast. The twins' hearts were beating nervously. *This is it. We are here at last.*

The ship edged its way into the harbour. A ragged and impromptu welcome party gathered on the quay: ships seldom managed to navigate the treacherous rocks around the island and visitors were rare.

"They don't look dangerous," Tancred said. He had fretted all the time the ship had been in the power of the current, wondering what sort of reception awaited them. He focused a telescope on the crowd.

The twins felt him stiffen. "What is it?" they asked.

"Guards, I think," he murmured.

The guards were marching through the streets of the harbour town towards the quay. They were like giant scorpions with human faces, hideous and frightening. They had strong jaws and red eyes; over their heads and shoulders flowed manes of tiny scarlet tentacles. They moved rapidly on six legs, waving claw-like hands. Having read about such creatures, he knew they had deadly stings in their tails – and that they were in the service of the Queen.

"Can't we stop this ship?" Tancred called down in

desperation to the captain. The captain shook his head helplessly.

Tancred turned to his children. "I'll go ahead in the boat," he said. "You stay here until I call for you." It was on the tip of his tongue to add, "And if I don't come back..." but he stopped himself just in time.

The twins watched their father row towards the harbour. They knew nothing yet of the scorpion-guards, but, reading the anxiety in their father's face, they felt very uneasy.

"I don't like the look of this," said Keiron.

"Nor I," said Cassie.

What are you thinking, Will? Keiron asked telepathically. He was talking to his little wooden manikin, who was sprawled half-hidden in his hair. Back in the days before they even had an inkling of their quest to find the Golden Armour, he had carved Will out of a piece of willow he had found in the woods. Cassie, with her miraculous gift for bringing creatures to life, had transformed him into a living being. Will had lived through all their trials and triumphs on North Island, and Keiron would be lost without him now.

I suggest you take a very long drink, said Will. *For there's an awful lot of thirst on that island – and soon you will feel it.*

Keiron took heed and went below to fill his water-bottle.

Cassie followed him, but she had other things on her mind. She unfolded a wolf-skin and stroked it unhappily. It had once belonged to Tara the wolf-girl, who had died at the hands of the monstrous

Child, trying to defend Cassie. Should she take the skin with her, as a comfort? She stroked it, and it made her feel calmer. In her mind's eye, the wolf-girl's almond-shaped eyes were watching her. Reluctantly she tucked the wolf-skin away: she sensed it would be safer if left on board.

Back on deck, Keiron handed her a tankard of water and gulped at his own. Will ran down his arm and leaned into the tankard to have his own sip. *We don't know when we'll get another one*, he said.

As Tancred's boat drew near the quay, the crowd grew more expectant. On his lap was the box which had once held the Golden Helmet; inside it he had put various items he thought might be useful as gifts or barter – fossils, polished stones, carvings, small books – but when he clambered on to the landing stage and held it up before him, all the crowd seemed interested in was water. "Water?" they said, jabbing at the box, a look of desperate hope in their eyes which puzzled him. When he shook his head, they scowled, muttered, or spat contemptuously at his feet. He opened the box, but no one seemed interested in its contents.

Behind him, several people jumped into the boat, pushing aside the two rowers. "Where is your water?" one of them demanded, and this was echoed by several others on the quay.

Tancred shook his head. He was beginning to understand: here there was, it seemed, nothing more precious than water. The sun beat mercilessly on everyone's heads, their tongues felt dry and swollen: they all craved for water. There were barrels of it on the ship, which the crew had replenished from a spring on Temple Island; and he understood at once the vulnerable position they were in.

Tancred's two rowers pushed a path for him through the crowd towards some camels which they guessed were for hire. There might just be time to get away before the scorpion-guards arrived. But even as they were bartering with the women who tended the camels, the milling crowd on the quay suddenly dispersed with amazing silence and rapidity, as if a gust of wind had swept them from the scene. The camel women shinned up their animals and turned the great beasts away.

Swinging around the corner from the town came the posse of scorpion-guards Tancred had glimpsed earlier in his telescope. Moving swiftly and decisively on their six whirring legs, their pincer-like hands pointing directly at the three men, their red eyes casting reflected beams of malevolent light, they surrounded Tancred.

One of them demanded, "Do you carry water on your ship?"

Tancred shook his head. In a flash the scorpion-guard's pincer-like hands were within inches of his face and its tail was swishing back and forth.

"You smugglers," the scorpion-guard sneered, "do you think we are so stupid as to allow you to bring in water so brazenly?" It turned to the other scorpion-guards and said, "Row over to the ship. Bring back all the water you can."

"No!" Tancred demanded, finding his voice at last.

"On this island you do as we say," the scorpion-guard snapped.

"But I thought the Queen ruled this island."

There was a perceptible pause before the scorpion-guard answered, its voice slightly less insolent. "That is so. All things are ruled by her. She and us."

"Then you should know that you are insulting one of her most distinguished guests," said Tancred, drawing himself up. He guessed how things stood, and the indignation he felt at being treated so roughly was beginning to overcome his fear of these ugly creatures.

"Oh, and who might that be?" said the scorpion-guard with another sneer.

"I am Lord Tancred, ruler of North Island," he declared, raising his voice. Several scorpion-guards paused and looked at him with curiosity. The scorpion-guard who spoke waved its two antennae in the air as if feeling for the truth of this claim.

Tancred looked into the ugliest face he had ever seen, eyes that seemed permanently angry and a mane that writhed at every movement. He tried not to show his inward shudder.

"No matter who you are," the scorpion-guard hissed, "no one, but no one, is allowed to smuggle water into East Island. Got that?"

"Even if it is a gift for the Queen?" Tancred retorted icily.

The scorpion-guard laughed. "She has all the water she could want," he said. "What would she want with yours?"

Tancred watched in dismay as the boat, full of bristling scorpion-guards, rowed towards the ship and his children.

*　　*　　*

The twins had viewed all this through telescopes. There was something horribly nightmarish about the slow progress of the boat as it came nearer and nearer, packed with those hideous creatures.

"Get up the crow's nest," one of the crew advised them. "We'll try and fight them off." The twins climbed up the rope ladder to the crow's nest, their hearts beating with fear, anxiety for their father as sharp as a knife.

The boat was a stone's throw from the ship when one of the rowers shouted to the crew, who were massed on the deck with various weapons ready, "Don't try and fight them. They'll sting us all to death."

The crew talked heatedly amongst themselves; but when the scorpion-guards leapt on to the deck one at a time, revealing a great springing strength in their legs, a few ineffectual blows, some arrows, and the stunning of one crew member with a light sting, were enough to make the crew back off.

Half the scorpion-guards followed some of the crew down below decks to the barrels of water. The bung was taken out of one barrel and the crew were horrified to see the water gush out. Desperately, the crew stood in front of the other barrels, pleading that the water should be spared. It was not the scorpion-guards' intention that the crew should die – the Queen had not ordered this – so they contented themselves with sniffing each barrel to check their contents. "If you are caught bartering this. . ." one of them warned, and by way of finishing the sentence, all the scorpion-guards clacked their claws together, a sound so horrible the crew felt sick with fear.

Up on deck, two scorpion-guards were contemplating the twins in the crow's nest. They tried shaking the mast to bring the children down. They tried leaping up, but they could not quite reach them. They hurled threats and missiles. They sent a crew member up to bring them down, but the twins shook the rope which he was climbing so hard he toppled off. None of these things succeeded in budging the twins, who clung to the crow's nest with grim determination.

Furious, a scorpion-guard seized a crew member and shouted at them, "Get down here now or I'll sting this man to death."

The twins looked at each other in dismay: they had no choice.